THE SPIDER:
CLAWS OF THE GOLDEN DRAGON

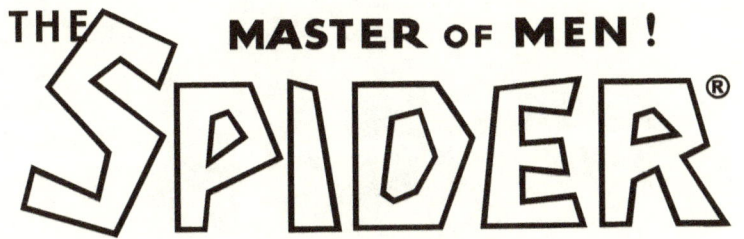

THE SPIDER

MASTER OF MEN!

CLAWS OF THE GOLDEN DRAGON

By Grant Stockbridge

POPULAR PUBLICATIONS • 2022

O N T H E day when the warning of the scarlet scorpion came to Richard Wentworth, he was enjoying one of the few periods of relaxation that fell in an over-crowded life. He was fencing with keen naked sabers before a gallery of friends in the gymnasium that occupied half the second floor of his fortified mansion between Sutton Place and the East River.

It was a colorful scene, with the cold sunlight of winter making gay yellow oblongs on the floor. Only the especially observant would have noticed that the glass in the tall windows was extra thick, bullet-proof, or would have guessed the constant peril that made this precaution necessary. There were few in the gallery who watched, and only one woman, but her vivid warmth, the quick flash of her intelligence, made her easily the dominant note of the entire scene. And it was she who first received the warning of the scorpion....

Wentworth and his adversary—his faithful man, Jackson— were stripped to the waist, without masks or plastrons, and the glittering blades were razor-sharp, without buttons.

They made a constant musical clatter in the hall.

Wentworth fought easily, his lean hawk's face relaxed in a faint smile that just showed the strong white line of his teeth. Jackson battled with a mounting fury of effort. Heavy jaw muscles knotted, he seemed massive and inordinately powerful against the slighter, lithe man who opposed him.

Wentworth's muscles glided with rippling smoothness in his tanned body, whose perfect symmetry was marred only by the cicatrices of a score of old wounds—wounds he had suffered in the service of humanity to which he long ago had pledged himself... to the struggle against criminal plot and counter-plot which ceaselessly thrust at civilization. Jackson was driving Wentworth back now, step after slow step. His saber made a constant clashing, its path marked by glittering arcs so swift they seemed continuous circlets of steel. Wentworth's smile had not changed, but Jackson's face showed increasing tension.

In the gallery, the woman fell silent and pointed with a small gesture of a white graceful hand.

"Watch," she said softly.

It came....

There was an abrupt change in the constant slithering clash of cut and parry. Wentworth's body seemed to weave with the sinuosity of a panther. With a ringing clatter, Jackson's saber sailed from his hand to strike point down, quivering, into the floor. Wentworth, his body extended in full thrust, remained motionless. His unguarded point just rested against Jackson's chest!

It was while the men who watched broke into applause, that a bearded and turbaned Hindu, moving on silent feet, glided to the side of the woman and offered a silver platter on which a small box reposed, a box of ebony and mother-of-pearl. His resonant voice was very subdued.

"One brought this to the master, *missie sahib*," the Hindu

murmured. "A Chinese. He said it was urgent, and now he has gone."

The woman stared down at the exquisitely-wrought box and a pallor crept up her cheeks while her rich lips still smiled.

So many times thus, in the midst of her rare pleasures with the man she loved and whose love she alone held, Nita van Sloan had received the call that would summon

The scientists, who had been summoned to the meeting, were now inhaling the death-spores!

him once more into the life-and-death conflict with powerful enemies. And, suddenly, she was… *afraid.*

Nita heard Wentworth's quiet, deliberate voice congratulating Jackson on his efforts; he was aware that Dick's guests were moving toward him while his butler, silver-haired Jenkyns, put a dressing-robe about his shoulders. She knew these things, but her eyes still held steadily upon the box on the tray.

"Very well, Ram Singh," Nita told the Hindu softly.

She lifted the box from the tray and, with caution born of long familiarity with danger, sprung the lid. Within, there was a lining of gold cloth and saffron silk. On it rested a figure wrought in vermillion and jade—a scarlet scorpion. It was a lovely thing yet, as Nita gazed on it, the smile finally left her lips.

Across the heads of the guests, Nita felt the touch of Dick Wentworth's eyes and her own, wide and dark with the sudden onslaught of a fear she could not analyze, met his with their message. She did not know the meaning of this scarlet scorpion, whether it was signal or warning, but in their lives such mysteries brought nothing save peril. Wentworth was suddenly at her side and Nita's gaze, brushing his face, found in its abruptly tautened lines ample confirmation of her fears!

Danger called.…

IT WAS not more than an hour later that, with the broad-shouldered Ram Singh at the wheel, Wentworth and Nita sped toward Chinatown in Wentworth's armored Daimler. They seemed a gay, social couple bound for an evening of pleasure, but there was a wariness in Wentworth's blue-gray eyes that scanned every building they passed and took account of each cross-street.

"The important thing—" he tried to speak casually to Nita at his side—"is to seem unsuspicious. I don't have any idea what is threatening in Chinatown, but I feel that Fu-Chang, whom I know, would have come to me, rather than send an anonymous warning—if there had been anything he could say openly. And if Fu-Chang, powerful as he is in the tongs, could not come openly, it must be something serious in the extreme! You can be sure of it."

Wentworth's keen brain was already actively seeking to pierce the secrecy which always veils dealings between West and East, and he admitted to himself that he was highly apprehensive. He had fought many master-criminals, but of all his battles, those in which men of the Orient had opposed him had been most frightful. The devious minds of the evil which the East occasionally spewed forth were without pity toward the white race. That some such new and secret enmity threatened, he did not doubt for a moment. For no other reason would his friend, Fu-Chang, have sent him so insidious a symbol as that scarlet scorpion....

Wentworth deliberately made his entrance into Chinatown as conspicuous as possible, driving to the entrance of the restaurant which was his and Nita's destination, with all the ostentation of his glittering limousine and the turbaned Sikh at the wheel. He wanted word of his presence to reach Fu-Chang. After that, he could depend on the subtlety of the Chinese to arrange the rest. For this reason, he devoted himself wholly to such a dinner as only the Orient could yield... and waited. He

5

and Nita were nearly finished when he noticed that their waiter was changed. The man who served them had given place to a Chinese girl—to the daughter of old Fu-Chang herself!

Wentworth realized this with a start that he barely concealed, and his apprehensions increased immediately. Surely, the message from Fu-Chang must be of transcendent importance that he could entrust it to no one except his cherished daughter—that he should be willing for her to demean herself in this way to bring the warning directly to Wentworth's ears! Wentworth glanced up into the girl's face and a cry sprang unbidden to his lips. He strangled it down, but his eyes made a single, swift sweep of the partitioned room in which they dined.

To the oblivious gay diners in the Dragon Inn, the girl's round face would have seemed placid, but Wentworth knew that she was rigid with terror!

"What is it, Hwang-yo?" Wentworth asked in a rapid undertone.

The girl shook her head faintly. "Not now, Wentworth *san*," she whispered. "There are those here who…" Her voice died, and Wentworth saw two blank-faced Chinese pad silently past the entrance of his booth. Their bead-black eyes merely brushed over Wentworth's face and passed on but, yet, instinctively, he tightened his arms against the twin automatics that nestled in shoulder holsters. Danger was here; danger naked and omnipresent. With hands that showed no slightest tremor, Hwang-yo lifted dishes from the table and moved toward the dragon screens to the rear behind which doors opened into the kitchen.

"Oh, what is it, Dick?" Nita whispered across the table to

6

Wentworth. "It's silly, of course, but I feel as if I were sitting over a mine that might explode at any minute."

"Laugh as if I were telling you a funny story," Wentworth cautioned in a low voice and, as Nita lifted her chin in false mirth, he hurried on. "Those two men who passed are *bow-how-dhoi*, hatchet men. I can tell by their hands and the characteristic walk—and one I've seen in action. You have your gun? Good. In the event—"

THE SCREAM came from the kitchen, a high, wavering cry of abject terror that ended in a bubbling cough, then aching silence. The laughter and gaiety of the dining-room switched off with the suddenness of a silenced radio. Over near the door, several guests sprang to their feet. With a leap, Wentworth cleared his seat and went bounding toward the screens behind which little Hwang-yo had vanished. Before he had taken two strides, those screens pitched forward, slammed to the floor, and toward him ran the daughter of Fu-Chang!

The girl ran swiftly, her head thrown back, her lips strained back against her teeth in flat terror. A high chatter of Chinese sprang up behind Wentworth, and his brain swiftly summarized the gist of it—even as he threw a protective arm about the girl. It was not hostile to himself. He understood in that brief instant that the menace came from outside; that they were as puzzled as himself by this sudden outburst of horror… A touch on his arm told Wentworth that Nita was at his side. His own guns were

7

swinging toward those kitchen doors, now blankly revealed by the fallen screen. They were batwing half-doors and they still vibrated slightly from Hwang-yo's eruption. Below them, Wentworth could see the white-trousered legs of a man. They were contorted, but still. Beyond them, nothing moved.

"Watch my back," Wentworth said softly to Nita. "We'll move toward the outer doors. Ready, Hwang-yo?"

Slowly, closely-bunched, they moved across the elaborately carved dining-room. Yellow men flanked them, but they were friendly and it was plain that they were as ready to defend Hwang-yo as he himself was. Fu-Chang was powerful... But these evidences of Fu-Chang's strength only increased the menace of whatever thing threatened the tong leader. It must be of incredible power if, even with the support of his countrymen, Fu-Chang needed to call on Wentworth for help!

Wentworth had almost reached the outer door when the sound came. It was incredible, unearthly, stunning in its mystery and blood-chilling violence. It was a scream, but surely such a scream as no man ever uttered—as no modern human ears had ever heard! It was such as human beings might conceive only in a dim and primordial past when great reptiles roamed the earth. For that scream was the hissing, tortured shriek of....

"The Dragon!" a Chinese moaned. "*The Dragon speaks!*"

On the instant, Wentworth found himself standing alone against whatever horror threatened from the bowels of the building. The Chinese had faded, vanished like mist from the face of a mirror, while what they called the Voice of the Dragon still sounded. The half-doors of the kitchen trembled faintly,

but that was all. Wentworth felt his nerves draw as taut as violin strings. The white guests of the restaurant suddenly broke into flight. Women screamed and men were white-faced and panic-stricken, darting for the exits. But no attack came; nothing came... Only Hwang-yo's hand plucked at his arm, weakly, with as little purpose as an infant's. His head whipped toward the girl. Her blandly round face was puckered between bewilderment and pain....

It was at this moment that Wentworth's eyes caught movement against the farther wall of the room. His glance flashed there and hung on the girl who stood beside a screen which plainly hid another doorway. She was slender with the litheness of the East, her body showing rounded curves beneath her dress of shimmering black silk. There was no color at all in her face, save for the vivid red of her mouth and, thrust into her hair, an orchid whose petals were violently red, were the sinister shade of blood....

While Wentworth stared, Hwang-yo uttered a pitiful little moan that turned into an incredible, throat-tearing scream. Wentworth wrenched toward her and saw her face, terribly contorted with some inner agony. Hwang-yo bowed slowly, tautly forward and collapsed in a writhing heap on the floor! Nita stooped over her, trying to find the cause of her seizure, and a word fought its way through the incoherence of the moans.

"The Orchid! The Blood Orchid!"

FOR A long moment, the words failed to register in Wentworth's brain, then he whirled toward the figure of the woman with the red orchid in her blue-black hair. The woman herself was gone, but in the spot where she had stood, the sinister parasitic flower lay, like a drop of blood, upon the floor! Wentworth crossed the room in swift strides and with a thrust of his arm swept aside the screen. He lunged through the revealed doorway—and brought up against a solidly built wall which did not yield at all to his charge!

Wentworth flung a swift glance around him, realized that he had plunged into a small closet. With the discovery, he hurled himself instantly backward—and not a moment too soon. Sliding in oiled grooves, a plate of steel clanged down across the doorway, filling it completely and sealing the closet as effectually as a vault! The steel panel exactly matched the wall. Wentworth pivoted, his eyes seeking some means of following that woman who had appeared so fleetingly, so terribly.

Nita's face, bent over the writhing Hwang-yo, was white and drawn. In the exit doorway loomed the tall, turbaned figure of Ram Singh.

Ram Singh swept a salaam, "The street fills with yellow men, *sahib!*" he called in his resonant nasal voice.

Wentworth nodded curtly, "Carry the girl to the car, Ram Singh," he said. "Nita, keep your gun in your hand and precede Ram Singh down the steps!"

With the words, he was past the Sikh and racing toward the street. There was a sharp crease between his eyes. He could make nothing of the terror of the Chinese or Hwang-yo's seizure, but he did know that when Chinatown fled at a sound, some new and awful menace was at work. Fu-Chang's summons had already told him that. Hwang-yo must be rushed to medical aid. After that, he would make his way directly to Fu-Chang and find the answer to this mystery of the dragon that screamed and the purport of this Blood Orchid!

In long strides, Wentworth hurried to the street below. His guns were ready in his fists, but in the narrow passageways of Chinatown, he found no menace. The walks and driveways were jammed with men and their high-pitched voices were lifted in a wavering chant. Their faces were upturned toward the heavens, their hands lifted in stricken petition. Wentworth checked in amazement, listened to the sing-song words:

"Oh, many-blazing dragon! Oh, bringer of the-death-that-flowers, spare us! Spare your slaves!"

Over the heads of the little praying men, Wentworth's amazed gaze caught sight of some of the police posted constantly here. Their faces, in the flickering red glare of neon signs, were as puzzled, as incredulous as his own. It was an unbelievable scene. Here within the shadow of New York's skyscrapers—within a few hundred yards of the center of a great western city's government—these men of the East were praying for salvation from some superstitious terror.

It was not in Wentworth's nature to know personal fear, but despite his certainty that some evil creature, hostile and criminal in intent, was behind all this, he felt a certain premonitory chill creep along his limbs. He knew it for what it was, the communicated dread of these hundreds of abject human beings. But it took a wrench, an effort of will to shake it off. At least he could be certain that, upstairs there, it had been some *man-made* mechanism which had almost taken his life!

He jostled through the close-pressed, unresisting ranks of men to his car, made a path as Nita and Ram Singh hurried after him, bearing the contorted body of the afflicted Hwang-yo. Wails of grief and fright went up from the close-pressed ranks. Distantly, Wentworth caught the fretting of police sirens, like the whimpering of frightened hounds.

"Behind the wheel, Ram Singh," Wentworth snapped. "Head for Bellevue. We've got to get this girl to medical care at once! These men must give way!"

Nita climbed in beside the Chinese girl in the armored tonneau of the Daimler, and Wentworth sprang to the running-board.

"Make way!" he shouted. "Make way for the stricken daughter of Fu-Chang! Make way, I tell you!" He repeated his orders in explosive Chinese.

But even when the powerful Daimler nudged them, they did not move. Their hands were lifted toward the heavens and they did not even seem to hear him. Wentworth began to toss men bodily aside, and the car moved slowly forward. Tightness lined his jaw. The feeling of menace, which had chilled him at the sight of these packed masses of humanity, grew steadily. He had fought Chinese criminals before this—men who for a while had held the fate of the entire nation in their grasp. But never had he seen the masses of Chinatown so completely enslaved. If this was some new monster who aimed at Western conquest....

WENTWORTH'S THOUGHTS cut short then, for once more, seemingly from the heavens themselves, came that hissing shriek. It was of such incredible proportions that it seemed to beat upon Wentworth's brain and body with actual physical violence. At the same instant, he became aware of tiny fragments like whirling leaves that drifted down into the upward reach of light-glow from the myriad signs of the streets. They were everywhere and, at sight of them, a wail of horror, such as was heard even above that awful shriek, rose from the assembled multitude.

As one man, the Chinese hurled themselves to the earth and began to bump their heads upon the pavement in the abject kowtow which the enslaved Chinese had used before the dragon throne of her conquering emperors! When those fluttering leaves touched men, they screamed and writhed in an agony that was either fear or actual pain. Wentworth did not know which. One of them brushed his sleeve and hesitated there for an instant before it drifted down to earth. Wentworth's eyes widened in amazement, for it was the petal of a red flower, a petal of... the Blood Orchid!

The Daimler had jerked to a halt. Short of crushing the prostrate men behind the wheels, there was no way of getting through the street. At Wentworth's signal then, Ram Singh sprang from behind the wheel and moved toward the tonneau. They could at least carry the girl afoot until they were clear of Chinatown and reached a taxi... Wentworth whirled toward

13

the car at an outcry from Nita. There was no fresh menace that Wentworth could see, but Nita, her face deadly pale, sprang to the ground and ran into his arms.

"The orchid!" she stammered. "The red orchid...."

In a leap, Wentworth reached the open door of the Daimler, then he paused while rage turned his eyes to glacial hue. The muscles worked along his jaw. For Hwang-yo lay sprawled on the seat upon her back, the throat of her dress burst asunder. Where her soft breast showed was a full-flowered bloom of the Blood Orchid! Its lush green stalk had... *sprouted upward from the girl's flesh!*

CHAPTER 2
THE DRAGON'S CLAW

WENTWORTH FOUGHT down the instant revulsion which the sight of that sinister bloom inflicted in him. He hurled himself to his knees beside Hwang-yo. His first impulse was to strike that horridly-growing parasite from her soft flesh, but he could not guess the consequences of such an act... At once, he saw that Hwang-yo was beyond his help, dead.

Rigid anger drew Wentworth to his feet. Fu-Chang's daughter had died in the attempt to fulfill a mission for her father, on Wentworth's behalf—and the power against which she had borne warning had struck her down before she succeeded. Plainly, Fu-Chang, himself, was in awful danger. There was no time to be lost. Wentworth must go to the aid of his Chinese friend!

14

He swung the girl's body into his arms, stepped to the street. "Ram Singh, take the *missie sahib* home!" he ordered curtly. "Full precautions!"

Nita caught her breath. She had not needed Wentworth's words ordering his mansion double-guarded to inform her that Dick was plunged once more into a life-and-death battle with the evil forces that periodically rose against the people he loved and voluntarily served. She ran to his side.

"No, Dick!" she cried. "We can't leave you unprotected here! You don't know how powerful this enemy can be. We're going with you!"

Wentworth's eyes met hers and he saw instantly that argument would accomplish nothing. There could not have been the strong affinity between them if her courage and strength had not been a close match for his own. Besides, there was no time... He nodded his assent and strode ahead, the apex of a flying wedge, while Nita and Ram Singh flanked him with ready weapons in their hands.

Wentworth's eyes were everywhere at once, scanning the still prostrate men for warning of any new attack. The shriek of the sirens was close at hand, but presently they would die, for not even riot squads of police could force their vehicles through the unresisting bodies of these men. There was no help that way....

Some part of the devious underground warrens of Chinatown Wentworth knew—at least, those portions which would lead him to Fu-Chang's side. He turned presently into a shop whose dusty windows were festooned with strings of dried herbs and other unmentionable things which, to the Chinese, constituted

RICHARD WENTWORTH

medicaments. With long, hurrying strides, he brushed aside
the curtains at the rear which partitioned off the living quar-
ters of the owner. There was no one here, and the only evidence
of recent occupancy were smoldering joss sticks before a small
shrine.

"Fu-Chang!" Wentworth whispered, and pressed against a bright hanging of silk.

The solid wall yielded to his pressure, actuated by electrical mechanism and the sonics of his carefully-pitched words. A narrow passageway, dimly lit at wide intervals by pale yellow bulbs, was revealed. Along this, Wentworth hurried. His feet made no echo, but the whisper of garments against the close walls was mockingly loud. Voices seemed to murmur in the distance, but there were no words, and there, in the middle of the narrow way, was a single ominous red petal—a petal of the Blood Orchid…Wentworth began to run.

The passage made a right-angle turn; steep stairs opened beneath Wentworth's feet. He took them in two long leaps, heard Ram Singh and Nita plunging after him. Another right-angle turn and he was racing across a cellar whose walls were dark-splotched with dampness. The whispering of voices was louder now, unmistakable. They rose and fell in a low-pitched chant. The black mouth of a doorway, framed in broken masonry, lay ahead, and new alarm sprang into Wentworth's heart, turned his throat dry with apprehension. That opening had been closed by a barrier, now ripped away!

At the discovery, Wentworth dropped to his knees, a warning cry on his lips for Nita and Ram Singh. Not an instant too soon!

From that black archway, the crimson-streaked yellow lance of gun flame leaped toward him. The bullet hummed viciously close to his head! Nita eased the body of Hwang-yo swiftly to earth, heard the swelling thunder of guns as Nita and Ram Singh both fired at the lurking assassin. Then Wentworth's own swift guns leaped to his hands.

The concussion in those narrow confines was stunning in its force, and other streaks of fire were blazing out ahead. Their lurid light illumined the masonry walls, the ceiling caught forming drops there with transient glittering points of brilliance! Wentworth sprang forward on the instant, the guns belching in both his hands, kicking against his stiffened wrists.

"After me!" he shouted. "Quickly! This is a death-trap!"

The thunderous roll of his weapons blew back the crouching assassins in the archway. A single bullet plucked at his left sleeve, but he scarcely felt it, did not heed it at all. In two long leaps, he had reached the cover of the wall. He thrust a gun through the opening and swiveled it like a machine gun. There were high-pitched screams, then the shuffling of retreating feet. Nita and Ram Singh bolted past him, and he heard the war-cry of the Sikh as he bounded in pursuit. Wentworth hurled himself through—and just in time. Those gathering drops from overhead were falling like a fearful rain.

Wentworth choked back a muffled oath as something that stung him with sudden agony struck the back of his left hand. He swept it clear, peered back into the chamber they had fled. Where those drops fell, spirals of vapor lifted. He saw them strike the body of Hwang-yo and, before his very eyes, her flesh

began to melt away! Chok-
ing fumes of... *of acid!*

Ram Singh's clear shout
came to his ears, "The way
is clear, master!"

Wentworth's lips drew
thin and cold against his

teeth. Awful to see that poor child's body mutilated, but there
was nothing he could do against that lethal rain from above. The
fumes were strangling him. He thrust Nita ahead toward the
sound of Ram Singh's voice, yet paused an instant beside the
men his bullets had felled. Chinese, they were; strong-thewed
men of the Northern provinces.

Wentworth's eyes narrowed as he stooped with a thin, platinum cigarette lighter in his hand.

He ground its base against the forehead of one of the dead. At
least, his unknown enemy should recognize that he had struck
at a foe who would battle back to the last moment of life!

WHEN WENTWORTH raced on, he had left a signature
behind—a signature glowing with the same blood-hue of the
petals of that deadly flower which had sapped out Hwang-yo's
life. It was a figure of sprawling hairy legs and poison fangs—
the seal of the Spider!

Few were the times when Wentworth, in his own identity,
had employed that dread symbol of the secret nemesis of the
night who turned his hand forever against the cohorts of the
underworld! Few were the people who knew that he was secretly
that lone wolf of justice who struck down those criminals whom

the law could not reach, or was too impotent to strike down. Nita knew, the one woman in the world who shared his every secret; also Ram Singh and his other faithful servitors. It must be closely guarded, for against the Spider the hand of every criminal was turned; and the law which he so valiantly defended hunted him, too.

For Wentworth never stopped in his swift vengeance to permit the slow, uncertain workings of the law to do its work. Too often, there was insufficient evidence for the ponderous machinery of legal punishment to overtake the offender. The Spider, himself, was judge and jury and executioner! Well might criminals tremble at his dread signature; well might this new and hidden monster, who could inflict death, pause and take heed lest the vengeance which had never failed now seek him out!

Instants later, Wentworth overtook Ram Singh and Nita where they stood against the blank brick wall which apparently ended the passageway. Wentworth paused and made a swift count of the bricks, pressed in hard upon a certain one, then guided it sideways as it yielded. Overhead, a small trap opened and Wentworth thrust his gun muzzle through it, twisted it twice to the right, once to the left. A doorway opened in the bricks, and Wentworth leaped through, to confront a steel door.

Once more, through it, he caught the rising and falling of the low-pitched chant which, by some fluke of the corridors, he had heard previously in that distant room of death. Wentworth began to strike on the steel with his bare fist… in a rhythm that produced a vibration. Its pitch started on a low note, rose slowly until it hummed like a temple gong. The steel lifted slowly and

Wentworth stepped through, quietly, his face in a harsh, stern mold.

Cross-legged on the floor sat his friend, Fu-Chang, and around him, prostrate, foreheads to the earth, crouched his servitors. It was their chant which had reached out through underground warrens to Wentworth's ears.

Fu-Chang lifted a face that was like old parchment, wrinkled and drawn. The eyes were dull, without animation. There was a flicker of recognition there, no more.

"My friend," his thin, worn voice barely reached Wentworth's ears. "My friend, you come too late. Flee while there is time!"

Wentworth motioned Ram Singh and Nita to stand guard by the door and crossed to the old Chinese's side, slid down into a cross-legged seat beside him.

"Fu-Chang," he said. "My news is heavy...."

A waved hand silenced him. "What you would say, I already know, my son," whispered Fu-Chang. "I shall not long outlive my grief. Listen! An evil one whose name is unknown to me has come to these shores to conquer. He brings such weapons as the world has never known! His plans, I do not know, save that he will enslave thousands to serve his ends. He begins tonight with twelve men of the Chinamerc company. I think he has already mastered the police... No, no, wait! My time is brief. You must be swift, or be too late. I... I...."

The withered lips opened, but the sound that came forth was no intelligible word. Fu-Chang's face worked with the effort. "The... The..." English was too difficult. He lapsed into his native Chinese. "Moyru Fei-pung... the Blood Orchid..." He slumped slowly forward, and the wails of the Chinese soared to a death keen.

WENTWORTH CAUGHT his friend into his arms—the friend who had been faithful to his loyalty even to the death of his daughter and himself. Rage drew Wentworth's nostrils thin and put ice into the gleam of his eyes. He lifted the old man's body and turned toward the curtained alcove bed against the far wall. He was scarcely aware of the instant flight of the servants, fleeing with high shrieks of fear through the corridors.

He brushed aside the curtains to lay the old man to his rest and a cry sprang to his lips. There in the accustomed shrine niche behind the bed was the familiar statuette of Buddha, but this was a new and awful representation of the Lord of the Lotus. For the Gautama no longer sat, placid and contemplating, upon the lotus flower. Instead, the bloom that enfolded him was hideous, blood-red—the bloom of the orchid!

Wentworth swept the offending thing from its niche and composed his friend's body upon the bed. What had been the cause of his death, he did not know. Some subtle poison, possibly. One thing remained certain. There was no doubt of the author of this second murder in the family of Fu-Chang. The Spider would take a many-fold vengeance when he had tracked the butcher to earth.

Wentworth drew the curtains, turned to face Nita and Ram Singh, still standing guard over the doorway, and in that same instant a voice spoke through the chamber of death—a voice that had the same hissing, harsh intonation of the scream of the Dragon!

"It is well that you have proclaimed yourself, Spider—little squirming insect!" it said. "You are my prisoners! Throw yourselves upon your faces and worship, that you may know *the mercy of the Blood Orchid!*"

For an instant after that awful voice spoke, Wentworth stood as if frozen, but he was not idle even for that brief while. In a single swift circuit, his eyes took in the entire room, to seek the source of that voice. The intensity of the tones in this confined space had confirmed his earlier guess that electrical amplification was employed to magnify it many times. Which meant that the speaker himself could be any distance away. Wentworth did not doubt that, however far off the leader himself was, the menace he voiced was omnipresent!

"Quickly!" Wentworth snapped. "Back the way we came!"

Ram Singh whirled instantly toward the entrance and sent the white beam of a flashlight probing into the darkness.

Nita placed her hand on Wentworth's arm. "The acid room!" she gasped. "We could never cross that!"

Wentworth nodded. "I'm counting on them to think exactly that!" he agreed and, with a sweep of his arm, knocked out the room's only electric light. Instantly, save for the white blade of light from the Sikh's flash, utter blackness descended. Wentworth threw an arm around Nita's waist and urged her toward the exit.

"If their leader were with them," he said softly, "it would be best to stay and fight it out here. But he's an Oriental—there's no mistaking that intonation. He'll stay well in the background. We've got to escape from here and warn Kirkpatrick.

This damnable organization of the Blood Orchid is planning mass murder or worse this very night!"

They were past the steel door and the brick barrier now and the damp walls pressed close to them. Ram Singh's light was just ahead.

"Master!" Ram Singh's clear voice held a note of doubt. "Master, there are… things in our path!"

Wentworth was at the Sikh's shoulder in an instant, his steadying hand clamping firmly on his man's arm. "Things?" he asked quietly, and then he saw the… *things*.

Everywhere before them glowed tiny spots of light, like the glinting reflection of mica, two by two. They were on the ceiling, on the walls and floor. Even as Wentworth paused with caught breath, he heard a faint, metallic rustling from the darkness. He whipped out his own flash, sent light probing at those tiny glittering points of light. Some faded away before the probe of the beam, but he caught sight of loathsome, hairy bodies.

"Spiders!" he whispered. "There's a scorpion… Tarantulas!" He laughed harshly. "Our friend of the dragon voice is pleased to be sardonic! Now, I know he's Oriental. Setting spiders to catch the Spider!"

There was no slightest tremor in his voice, though he realized that death lurked before them at the fangs of anyone of those noxious creatures. Only one thing was in their favor. All the killers were nocturnal and disliked the light. They would retreat before the flashlights, but there were a myriad crevices into which they could dart. If one lurked behind and sprang upon them unawares… Nita, in her silken evening dress and cloak was the most exposed.

Her silken ankles… Wentworth swept her up into his arms.

"Go ahead, Ram Singh," he ordered quietly. "Your light will drive them back. But see that you drive them *all* back. Go slowly. Anyone of them can cause almost instant death!"

NOTHING OF the impatience that goaded Wentworth showed in his voice. They must creep to avoid noisome death, and meantime, mass-murder was being prepared by the Dragon. Wentworth's eyes darted everywhere as they advanced, watching the crevices. Abruptly, the gun he carried in his right hand blasted, and brick dust flew from the ceiling above Ram Singh's head. There was a smear where a moment before a tarantula had been about to drop on the valiant Sikh!

"Steady," Wentworth spoke quietly. "Only another fifty feet!"

His eyes strained ahead along the corridor. If the bodies of the Chinese they had slain already had been removed… He drew in a short, thankful breath. He could catch the faint reflection from their clothing. There were no more of the gleaming eyes ahead now. In another few moments the gauntlet of death would have been run. They… The dark thing dropped without a sound from the ceiling and on the back of Wentworth's hand, clenched about Nita's shoulders, a small scarlet scorpion rested, its tail lifted, quivering in the air—ready to strike!

Nita smothered a scream, and the lineaments of Wentworth's face drew into more stern lines. "Ram Singh!" he said sharply. "On my side… *shoot!*"

Ram Singh whirled and his fine dark eyes dilated. His gun

swung into line with the speed of light, and the blast beat against their ears thunderously—but the scorpion was gone. Across Wentworth's hand was a black streak of powder burn. His lips moved in a brief smile.

"Thanks, warrior. Now, swiftly. Those dead men will make us a bridge across the chamber of acid!"

Nita's eyes closed but a smile played faintly about her lips as they hurried on. "I can walk now, Dick," she said. "There are no more of those horrid beasts."

Wentworth brushed his lips across her hair. Her courage was a thing that did not need proof, but she was incomparably dear to him now. He knew how her very soul would shrink from the thing they must do.

"Careful, Ram Singh," he said steadily. "Put that light out and keep behind the wall as much as possible. They may be lying in wait on the farther side of the room."

The crossing of the acid chamber was a horror, but it was quickly accomplished and, on the other side, Wentworth drew a deep breath of relief.

"Now! A short dash and we can race for police headquarters!" he said. "We must reach Kirkpatrick before...."

He did not finish the sentence. The horrors that he knew were threatening needed no articulation for emphasis. They still went cautiously, but with increased speed and Wentworth took the lead now, with Nita between himself and Ram Singh. He needed his keen eyesight, his sure memory. Men who had had time to plant that horror of death along their path could easily have rigged some new trap here. They might have utilized some of those which Fu-Chang must surely have built as a protection for his dwelling, but left unset except in time of stress.

Far ahead, a faint beam of light showed, marking the beginning of the electric lights which led back to the shop of the Chinese pharmacist. He could see the steps. Wentworth lengthened his pace, yet redoubled his observation. They must be almost within earshot of the many police who undoubtedly still thronged the street....

He stopped to survey the steps carefully. Nothing seemed wrong with them, but he was suspicious. It would be like the irony of the Chinese to spring their trap now when the victims believed themselves at last within reach of safety.

"I'll go first," Wentworth said quietly. "Wait at the bottom until I have reached the top."

"Let thy servant go first!" Ram Singh cried, but Wentworth was already taking the steps with great leaping bounds. He reached the top, turned to smile assurance back at Nita... and then a great, rending cry burst from his lips. Even as he smiled down at Nita, the bottom of the passageway opened beneath her. In an instant, she and the valiant Ram Singh were plunged out of his sight—and the trap-door floor of the passageway had swung shut again.

From somewhere in the dim corridors, Wentworth caught the faint sound of hissing laughter—the laughter of the Dragon!

CHAPTER 3
KOWTOW OR DIE!

BLANK HORROR nailed Wentworth to the spot. He had thought to face the greatest danger himself by going first, and he had only sprung the trap which plunged Nita and Ram Singh into God alone knew what menace! The mechanism had been simple, obviously prepared so that a Chinese, leading an unwelcome guest along this corridor, could drop him through the floor. Well, the trap could be sprung again by the same method!

With the quickness of muscles grown rigid with apprehension, Wentworth hurled himself down the steps and along the corridor for a few paces, then turned and retraced his steps, exactly duplicating the movements which had plunged Nita and Ram Singh through the floor. As soon as he reached the head of the steps, he sprang outward in a leap that carried him to a stand upon the trapdoor and... *nothing* happened!

Once more, it seemed to Wentworth, the hissing sound of that mocking laughter echoed through the subterranean corridors. Anger surged through Wentworth. His twin automatics were in his hands, muzzles questing for a target as he stared downward at the stubborn trap beneath his feet. No thought of fear for himself was in his mind—no dread of the horror into which he might instantly plunge. He cared only to follow Nita, to track down if possible the monster who must be lurking somewhere near, or whose men could be followed.

No, he couldn't fire at the catches of the trap. Nita and Ram

Singh might be still beneath him. But the hinges… Even as the thought glanced across his mind, the automatics were speaking, hurling their heavy slugs with a force of a quarter ton against the hinged side of one leaf of the trap. Distantly, he heard shouts— not from below, but from forward along the corridor… white men's shouts. Something that was almost a sob of thanksgiving swelled up through Wentworth's throat. That would be the police, drawn by the sound of his shots. He sent an answering call, urged them to hurry… but to be careful!

Deliberately, he continued to search the wood with bullets until he heard the ring of metal and knew he had found the hinge. He hurled the sledgehammer blow of his lead from both guns then, concentrating on that spot. Footsteps—heavy reassuring white footsteps—were pounding along the corridor….

"This way!" Wentworth shouted. "I'm Richard Wentworth. Two of my friends fell through this trap."

A sergeant of police, short, powerful police gun in his hand, ran to the head of the steps, and Wentworth gave a rapid explanation of the trap.

The sergeant turned his head. "Axes here!" he shouted. "And bring them hydraulic jacks! Sure, Mr. Wentworth, we'll be through that floor in a jiffy. Just you stand aside now!"

An instant later, blue-coated men bounded down the hall and at a curt gesture of the sergeant, began to slam their ax blades into the floor. The sergeant stood alertly beside Wentworth, his revolver ready.

"O'Hara is my name, Mr. Wentworth," he said. "I've seen you

many times about headquarters with
the Commissioner. A grand man, the
Commissioner."

"He's here?" Wentworth asked,
and heard the strain in his own voice.

"He'll be here," O'Hara said confi-
dentially. "Now, don't you be worry-
ing. We'll be through this floor in a jiffy."

Wentworth's eyes were riveted on the trapdoor. What would
they see when the floor was driven in? So many traps of the
Chinese led to death. There, were the pits of poisoned feathers
that swirled into a man's throat and nostrils and strangled him
horribly; pits of long spikes with needle points; pools of ancient
turtles with beaks like razors and that could take off an arm....

"Hit nearer the wall," Wentworth ordered sharply. "Tear the
hinges loose!" His feet worked inside his shoes, toes gripping
against the floor, ready to spring. God, could Nita still be... still
be alive and not answer the urgency of his voice?

"Who is it that's below there, sir?" O'Hara asked, his deep
cheerful voice a little muted at the drawn anxiety of Wentworth's
face. It was kindness that actuated him, striving to turn Wentworth's mind from the horrors that might be below. Wentworth
answered jerkily, eyes still searching, searching... Abruptly, a
blow of the ax drove a hinge loose. The policeman who was
wielding it wrenched it free, slung the blade down again—and
half the trap fell in!

INSTANTLY, WENTWORTH was at the edge, peering
down. His flashlight was immediately reinforced by O'Hara's...

but they revealed *nothing*. A corridor, yes, much like the one in which they stood and perhaps ten feet below, but nothing else. With an oath, Wentworth sprang over the edge, landed on sprung knees, eyes and light questing about. It was not a corridor, but a brief passageway, whose ends were blank walls of bricks. There would be a way through, a secret door, but hours might be spent in a vain search for the catch that would loosen their locks, unless he were lucky....

Wentworth strode to the farther wall and began to fumble with the bricks. There were three police in the pit with him now and, at O'Hara's orders, they assailed the other end of the passageway with crowbars.

"This is the way it always is, sir," O'Hara said heavily. "We break down one barrier and find a half dozen more. It's how the devils always get away from us, damn their heathen souls! It's beyond me how...."

A shout from the men working at the other end of the corridor whirled Wentworth that way. The crowbar that one of them wielded was wedged between bricks and, around them, dancing in the brilliant beam of the lights, was a thick reddish dust. Even as Wentworth watched, the man's hands dropped from the bar. He turned away, bent double, hands clutching at his throat, coughing, coughing terribly....

"Out of here!" Wentworth shouted. "Out, quickly!"

He cupped his nose and mouth in the crook of his elbow, held his breath while he flung an arm about the waist of the strangling man. Hands reached down eagerly from above, snaked them up. But other men were coughing now. The three who had been battering at the end of the passageway were stricken, racked by convulsions of strangulation. Their faces reddened, eyes started from their sockets. O'Hara bellowed an order, began to cough....

They were all four on the floor above now, and Wentworth, his head reeling from long-held breath, scrambled up beside them. He blew out his pent wind in a violent gust to clear his nostrils and throat, but even so he felt pain in the lining of his nasal passages. He leaned against the wall, coughing, eyes watering... but thanks to his precaution, the paroxysm passed. The other men were not so fortunate. They writhed on the floor, tearing at their throats with frenzied hands.

"Water!" Wentworth croaked hoarsely at the men who stood helplessly beside them. "Water! Wash out their mouths, noses, throats. Hurry, you fools! They're choking!"

The very flesh of their throats was swelling, empurpled with congested blood. One of the policemen doubled up in a last agony and blood seeped out between his clenched teeth. Then he was still, blessedly still—in death. But the others still were suffering. Wentworth knelt beside O'Hara, tried to relieve him. His swelling throat already had burst open his collar. Wentworth forced open his lips, and horror shook him. O'Hara's throat was completely closed by a fiery inflammation that had sprung into instant being at the touch of the red dust. Wentworth's own throat was painful, and his breath came raspingly, though his affliction had been slight. Even while he knelt, the last convulsion seized O'Hara and Wentworth pushed heavily to his feet. The others all were dead and the rest of the police, who had worked from the floor above, were shrinking away from them, faces white.

"Out of here!" Wentworth ordered hoarsely. "Take these men with you. Out, I say! Further search will mean only... further deaths!" Heavily, he followed the blue-coated men to the streets. Nita was behind him there; Nita and Ram Singh. But if they were alive, they already must have been borne far away. God, what could he do to save them! He had not the slightest clue to their captor other than the hissing scream of the dragon and the brief appearance of that fateful woman with the blood-hued orchid... But *wait!* Before he had died, Fu-Chang had mentioned an attack on "twelve men of the Chinamerc." That was an oil company, Wentworth knew, with great fields in China. His course was clear. Wentworth's face drew into harshly chiseled lines and the gash of his mouth was bitter. Yes, his duty was to go to the rescue of those twelve men. From them, or from an attack upon them, he might gain some clue to the whereabouts of the Dragon-man who had seized Nita and Ram Singh, If they had not been instantly killed in the trap, they would be spared for a while—spared to die more horribly later on! For to the Chinese of the ilk of the Dragon-man, torture was a fine art perfected with much practice—upon the unfortunates who fell into their power!

It was almost more than he could do to drive himself from the spot where Nita had vanished. Wentworth's very body seemed to protest the desertion. He must battle for clear thought to realize that, by leaving, he might find her the sooner. His eyes were suddenly haggard and there was a heavy weariness in all his fibers; his very bones felt tired and old… Defeat. That was what it was.

He had faced defeat before this in his battles with the under-world, but to meet such overwhelming defeat so early in the struggle, to be robbed of the woman he loved, upon whom he leaned for strength in his trials… Wentworth fought for the

He was performing the abject
kowtow of the East!

calm coldness, the bitter fire that had carried him through so many crises....

He drove himself to enter the Daimler, still standing where so short a while before he and Nita and Ram Singh had abandoned it, united then. For a long moment, he sat drooped over the wheel. Then he snapped up his head. There was work ahead and, perhaps, a vengeance! He spun the heavy car about and hurled it, with horn roaring, through the streets toward police headquarters. There he would find his old friend, Kirkpatrick, keenest Commissioner of the police that New York City had ever known. Together, they would plot the detection and destruction of this monster who threatened the city! Side by side, together....

WENTWORTH JERKED the car to a halt before the green lights in Centre Street and flung himself through the broad doors, barely acknowledged the salute of the man at the information desk. Kirkpatrick must be upstairs. He would never leave his office in time of crisis, such as he must have recognized in the alarms from Chinatown. Wentworth was conscious of a great need for Kirkpatrick, for his calm brain and his sympathy. For so many years, Wentworth had fought alone against the world. Now he was doubly alone, bereft at once of his strong henchman and of Nita... He swung into the outer office, and Kirkpatrick's police secretary sprang into his path.

"Sorry, Mr. Wentworth," he said, "you can't go in!"

Wentworth stopped short, staring at the man. It was a thing that had never happened before. Always, under all circumstances, he was given instant admission to the office of his friend.

Anger flared in Wentworth's eyes, but he fought it down. He was being silly. Probably, Kirkpatrick was in the midst of a conference. It was only the urgency of his own need that drove him so.

"In conference?" he asked, and the rasping hoarseness of his voice startled him.

The red-headed cop shook his head, with an apologetic smile. "No, sir, not in conference. Alone," the man said. "But he left orders nobody was to come in. He mentioned you by name, sir."

Wentworth's eyes narrowed in swift apprehension. This was not like Kirkpatrick, and falling as it did in the midst of this new menace! Good God! What was it that old Fu-Chang had said? *I think he already has mastered the police!* Oh, this was madness! Master Kirkpatrick? No criminal had ever aspired so highly!

But Wentworth's fears would not down. His mind raced back to that awesome scene in the streets of Chinatown, a horde of yellow men prostrate in the streets because some petals of red flowers had drifted down from the skies. The dragon voice? That was only some mechanical contrivance… So Wentworth told himself, but the pounding of his heart was loud in his temples and there was coldness about his heart.

"Listen, Dugan," he said softly, fighting down the panic that was rising in his breast. "Just what did the Commissioner say? Try to remember exactly."

Dugan's eyes widened a little at Wentworth's tone. "Why, sir, he just came to the door and looked out. He didn't exactly look at me, but kind of over my head or behind me somewhere. He said, "I am not to be disturbed the entire evening for anything. For anything at all, do you understand, Dugan? If Mr. Wentworth comes, tell him that. It's an order. If I'm disturbed, you're fired from the force. Understand?' It was kind of funny, now that you mention it."

"Funny!" Wentworth drew in a slow breath and moved toward the inner door of Kirkpatrick's office. He heard the low whir of the phone bell inside, heard Kirkpatrick's voice, muted by the walls, speak shortly. "Dugan, I'm going in!"

Dugan sprang back from him. "You can't, sir! I've got my orders!"

"Can't you understand, man! The Commissioner isn't well! He's... He's being forced to do what he's doing."

Dugan shook his red head stubbornly, "I got my orders, sir, and...."

"Confound it, Dugan!" Wentworth took a long stride toward the man, and the policeman made a fumbling gesture toward his gun. Wentworth leaped. He nailed Dugan's wrist to his side. "Don't be a fool, Dugan. I'm going inside!"

Dugan struggled with him, and Wentworth brought a chopping fist to the man's jaw, eased him to the floor. He took a long stride to the door and, hand on the knob, hesitated. Now that the way was clear... He could no longer hear Kirkpatrick's voice inside. He could hear nothing. Wentworth drew in a quick breath, and thrust open the door, sprang inside at the same instant. Then he swore, hoarsely and terribly, staring at the scene within.

Kirkpatrick was on his knees at the end of the desk. He was bent far forward, bumping his forehead on the floor, heavily, ceremoniously. He was performing the abject kowtow of the

East and before him… *was a tiny statuette of Buddha, seated upon a Blood Orchid!*

CHAPTER 4
TWELVE DOOMED MEN

S ICK DISMAY laid its heavy hand upon Wentworth. This could not be Kirkpatrick, his friend, the strongest and most incorruptible man who had ever headed New York's great police department! It could not be, but it was. Humbly beating his head upon the floor before the heathen representation of the power of the Dragon-man!

With a furious oath, Wentworth snatched up the statuette and hurled it crashing through the window. For an instant, lifting his head, Kirkpatrick stared at him in amazement and Wentworth saw that his eyes were strained as wide as a sleep-walker's. The pupils were fearfully dilated, sightless. Then Kirkpatrick was on his feet, with a shout of rage. In a long leap, the Commissioner reached his desk, ripped open a drawer and seized his long-barreled revolver.

A sob in his throat, Wentworth sprang in and struck in one smooth flow of action. His fist clicked audibly to the jaw, and Kirkpatrick was spilled across his desk. His muscles went lax then and he slumped slowly to the floor while Wentworth stood staring, still shaken with the horror of the thing he had witnessed. He had come to Kirkpatrick for help and instead he was confronted with the spectacle of a completely subjected man. Truly, as Fu-Chang had said, the police department was already mastered!

It could not continue. That dilation of the eyes meant clearly that Kirkpatrick was either drugged, or hypnotized—possibly both. Flashing across Wentworth's brain was the memory of that phone call which had been coming in while he spoke with Dugan. Wentworth leaped to the phone and, dropping his voice to the clipped, metallic intonation which Kirkpatrick used, spoke crisply over the wire.

"Put a tracer on that last call on my wire," he ordered. "Call me as soon as you have information. Also, get hold of Doctor Ridley for me and have him come to my office at once. An emergency!"

He hung up and bent over his friend, flicked up an eyelid. Whatever fearful power dominated the Commissioner still was in force. The eyes still held that fixed, wide-pupiled stare, even in unconsciousness. With swift movements, Wentworth pulled Dugan into the inner office also, bound and gagged him. There must be no interruption until he had completed his task here. Time was racing away from him; time in which he must act or lose Nita forever—and lose the battle to this super-criminal out of the East!

Swiftly, still using Kirkpatrick's voice tones, he got in touch with his own home and ordered the place into a state of siege; commanded Jackson to come with all speed to headquarters. With his own intimate knowledge of the working of the police then, he threw up what safeguards he could against the still-un-detected purposes of the Dragon-man.

If only Kirkpatrick were himself! By a swift survey of the reports of the day, a few brief questions at key points, the Commissioner might be able to put his finger on the danger spots. He knew so well the ordinary course of crime within the city that any slight change would be at once perceptible! It was a damaging blow that the Dragon-man had struck!

When Dr. Ridley, Wentworth's personal physician, arrived, Wentworth had completed what precautions he could take. He had also ascertained that the board of directors of the China-merc company comprised just twelve men as Fu-Chang had indicated! It was meeting this very night; in fact their session already had got under way.

Wentworth tried to get through to them by telephone but it was futile. But of what use would a phone call have been? Against what and whom could he warn them? For all Wentworth could tell, the enemy might be one of their own number! The whirring phone jerked Wentworth's attention to it, but it was only the sergeant's report of failure to trace the Dragon call. Wentworth turned with an oath to where Dr. Ridley bent over the still-unconscious Kirkpatrick.

"You're right," Ridley growled, shaking his massive head. "It's a narcotic of some kind, but I haven't penetrated the secret yet. You hand me the damnedest problems, Wentworth. Why in the hell I help you...."

"Take him to your hospital," Wentworth snapped. "I'll help you get him out of here. I tell you, Ridley, there is terrific danger hanging over the city, and unless you can restore him to his proper senses...."

Ridley shrugged, "I'll do my best. Any idea how I'm going to get him out?"

Wentworth nodded curtly and, with swift precision, stripped off Kirkpatrick's clothing and Dugan's—put the guard's uniform on the Commissioner and, himself, donned Kirkpatrick's clothing. With the addition of Kirkpatrick's trim overcoat, his perpetual gardenia fastened to the lapel and the customary derby set precisely on his forehead, Wentworth thought that he would have no trouble in simulating Kirkpatrick's identity long enough to get Kirkpatrick himself out of the building. He turned to the window while the doctor summoned men with a stretcher.

"Dugan's been taken sick," he curtly told the sergeant over the phone. "I'm going to the hospital with him. Back soon."

It was no more difficult than that and, a moment after Dr. Ridley had sped away with Kirkpatrick, Wentworth sprang into the Daimler. In response to his phoned order, his man, Jackson, had taken over the wheel.

"**THERE WAS** a phone message at the house, sir," Jackson reported in his curt, military voice. "A funny kind of voice. Said, 'Inform Wentworth that if he wishes to spare himself pain, he will lock himself in his home and stay there.' The fellow talking said you need not fear him unless you got in his way. I tried to trace the call. Got nowhere."

Wentworth's lips pressed in upon themselves, but he made no response other than an acknowledgment of the message. No doubt what that meant at all. To an extent it was hopeful. It implied that Nita was still alive; that she would be a hostage for his good behavior! Wentworth's eyes grew thin and cold, but his mouth was twisted with pain. How many times in the past he had had this choice to make—his love for Nita or the duty which he had laid out for himself? But God knew and Nita knew, there could be no choice. She would have thrown the Spider's defiance at the Dragon-man even as Wentworth himself would have done. She would know that Wentworth would fight on, doubly-intent on triumph, because of that warning message... No, there could be no hesitancy in the choice, but the hurt was an ever-fresh wound. He must act, and act fast! If he stopped to think....

Wentworth's hands were steady as steel, as he touched the button which revealed the wardrobe hidden in the back of a half of the car's rear seat. He carefully drew the curtains of the Daimler, opened up a make-up tray with its illuminated mirror and, deftly, set to work upon his face.

A swiftly-applied fluid sallowed the skin and drew it tautly across cheekbones and the bridge of his nose. A few touches blotted out the lips and turned the mouth into a ruthless gash; the nose was transformed into a predatory beak. That was all— save for bushy brows, that changed the eyes to hollows, and a lank wig. No longer were the handsome, chiseled features of Richard Wentworth reflected. It was the sinister and ominous aspect of the Spider!

With that disguise, Wentworth drew danger about him like a glove. Every man's hand would be turned against him now, be he police or criminal. Yet it gave Wentworth this advantage—where he stalked in this garb, terror walked, too. Fear was a powerful ally. Heaven knew, he would have need of every support now!

He plucked up the speaking-tube that connected him with Jackson, began to talk swiftly of the events of the night. His eyes rested warmly on the stalwart shoulders of Jackson. They had fought side by side through the war, and each had saved the other many times; Wentworth as captain, then major—and Jackson his sergeant. Master and man, yes, but more than that—fast friends.

"We fight," Wentworth told him quietly, "against one of the most vicious and clever criminals I have ever faced. Remember that while you stand guard below. At the least suspicious circumstance, fire a rocket up past the windows—I'll be on the twentieth floor. If the threat comes from criminals, a red rocket. If from the police, green. If the danger is extreme, fire white. After that, use your judgment. Remember, if you, too, are seized, I must fight alone…" So Wentworth finished, knowing well that loyalty would be a more potent argument for caution with Jackson than any warning of personal danger which he might utter.

Wentworth peered ahead then and spotted the lighted windows of the Crofts building for which he was bound. On the twentieth floor there, twelve men were holding a meeting—and only Wentworth and the Dragon-man knew that they met in the very shadow of death. Wentworth drew a broad-brimmed black hat low over his brows, swung a long cape about his shoulders. What a human being could do to avert this tragedy, Wentworth would attempt, but there was another, deeper purpose underlying this trip. He must trap some minion of the Dragon-man when the attempt was made against the twelve—and wrench from the captive the whereabouts and identity of the Dragon-man himself!

At Wentworth's light tap on the glass, the Daimler swerved to the curb. The door opened, softly closed, and a darker shadow blended with the darkness against the building's wall, marking where the Spider made his swift and silent way....

ON THE twentieth floor of the Crofts Building behind ground-glass doors which bore the single legend *Chinamerc*, was a square, many-windowed room. Through those windows could be seen the distant harbor lights, the speckled shore of Jersey. The room's chairs were leathern, luxurious, and the deep-piled rug on the floor had come from ancient China. But none of the twelve men seated about its broad, gleaming mahogany table paid any heed to these things.

They seemed to see, to feel nothing at all. Each one sat bolt upright, eyes fixed straight before him. It was a fact that their seemingly sightless eyes were all focused on one point in the center of the table—a point occupied by a small statuette, a Buddha seated upon a blood-red flower....

The silence of the room was unbroken, for those twelve scarcely seemed to breathe. They, too, might have been statues, their strongly-hewed faces chiseled from unyielding stone. They were masters of finance, these men, but tonight they had met one greater than they... They sat silent and rigid and, if they even thought, there was no evidence of that fact upon their faces.

Presently, the man at the head of the table lurched to his feet. From the table before him, he picked up a sheet of paper upon which eleven names had been scrawled, one beneath the other. He folded that paper and thrust it into his pocket, then he prostrated himself upon the floor and struck his forehead three times. The thuds came dully through the thick pile of the rug. He got heavily to his feet.

"Master," he said thickly, "I come!"

He walked out of the room, but the other eleven remained as men graven from stone, still staring at the tiny Buddha in its scarlet flower cup. Minutes dripped past, and nothing stirred. Perhaps a man's face twitched; perhaps there was a little tremor in a hand, no more than that. Yet there was evil in that room, an evil that brooded with a heaviness of physical weight upon the hearts of those eleven motionless, doomed men....

A voice spoke in that room—a voice, though no man's lips moved. It came, if anywhere, from that tiny Buddha upon the table, but the voice was the hissing rasping tones of the Dragon-man! It spoke one word, and at its echoes, those eleven men vibrated like exactly-matched tuning forks. Terror tightened their eyes, but they did not move.

The word that rasped into the room was, *"Die!"*

Another minute dragged past. Then those eleven men lurched to their feet and one of their number turned rigidly in his tracks and stalked to a window which he flung high. A window through which the distant lights of the harbor, of the Jersey shore were visible, a window twenty stories above the earth. When he had raised that window, the man climbed upon the sill. His hands jerked at his sides. His head was wrenched backward. It twisted from side to side like a man who struggles impotently against a throttling hand at his throat. He fought, standing rigidly on the sill—fought against something that could not be seen, but which was as solidly and ominously in that room as if Death himself stood there with his grim, blooded scythe.

Once more, the *voice* spoke in the room, its single syllable of doom. *"Die!"* it said.

The man on the windowsill uttered a choked, pitiful cry, no more than a whisper in the immensity of the black night that yawned hungrily beneath his feet. He lifted a leg as rigid as iron and... stepped down out of sight. No cry came upward to mark his downward whirl through the blackness; no sound from the other ten men who waited their turn beside the window. Another man stepped to the sill, and the Buddha whispered, *"Die!"*

OUT OF the darkness of the void, a figure swung into sight, a figure from whose shoulders flapped a long cape, whose eyes burned from beneath bushy brows and whose hawk face was filled with menace. A long arm reached out and swept the man from the sill, back into the room, hurled him to the floor. On the sill stood the Spider, shoulders hunched in the pose the world had learned to know so well, and which a crooked underworld had come to fear as it feared not all the forces of the law.

"Fool!" rasped the Spider. "Fool, why would you kill yourself?"

The nine men still on their feet stood rigidly, unanswering. The other was dragging himself up from the floor where Wentworth had hurled him. None of them answered, but the Buddha whispered, *"Die!"*

As if Wentworth had not stood there, another of the men

47

stepped toward the window and attempted to mount the sill. If Wentworth had not been secured by the length of silken rope by which he had swung from the roof above, he might have been hurled to the street to his death then. But the rope served him well. He drove another of the men back from the brink of the death he courted for himself! There was a touch of horror in Wentworth's widened eyes. He had been a fool to think that the Dragon-man would come in person to wreak his fearful doom upon these doomed men!

"*Die!*"

Another stepped forward, then the others. All of them were crowding toward the window at once. Wentworth struck out with a swift, hard fist, but the man he hit seemed scarcely to feel the blow. They were crowding forward now, all intent on plunging to their death below at the behest of that whispering Buddha on the table. Wentworth fought violently to drive them back, while horror laid its cold fingers upon his heart. It was like fighting the living dead. His blows were futile and unless he hurled these madmen bodily from the window, they paid no heed to him. It was nightmarish, horrible.

"*Die!*"

A more active madness seized upon the men. They were being given orders which they must obey and which they could not obey, because of this black caped thing in the window. Wentworth saw anger leap into the eyes of the men he opposed, saw one of them draw a gun. It was laboriously slow, that draw. The Spider's guns could leap to his hands a dozen times while that man pulled his weapon, but the Spider did not injure the innocent.

These men were as much victims of the malign power that was grasping the reins of the city as was sweet Nita herself, plunged through that fateful trap into the hands of the Dragon-man. No, Wentworth couldn't fire on these men; but neither could he permit them to plunge to their deaths....

Violently, Wentworth hurled himself into the battle. He leaped from the sill and drove two of the men to the floor, but the others stumbled over him, their eyes fixed with the intensity of desire upon that open window and the death it offered. The Spider tripped them, threw them to the floor, piled man on top of man... and they rose again, to press past him, to thrust him aside—always groveling toward that window, goaded into a fury by that monotonous, fearsome voice that repeated in its hissing whisper the command, *"Die!"*

Even Wentworth's great strength was being drained by the futile battle against such hopeless odds. One of the men abruptly seized him by the shoulders and whirled him half-across the room and once more the phalanx of those eager to die converged on the window.

"Die!" croaked the voice from the Buddha. *"Die!"*

From where he lay, Wentworth glimpsed slim wires that dangled from beneath the table and, with a shout, he sprang upon the scarlet-throned Buddha, wrenched it free and hurled it across the room. He spun toward the men, and when the Spider spoke, it was in the hissing croak of the Dragon-man himself.

"Live!" he cried, *"Live! I bid you to live!"*

AS ABRUPTLY as if control wires had been snapped on, those poor marionettes bent on suicide, now ceased their struggles toward the window and stood, inanimate, rigid. Wentworth clung panting to the table and stared at them. There were only nine left. Nine… Then three had plunged to their deaths below! But Wentworth had seen only one leap before he had swung down from the roof to rescue them against their own will. One must have leaped just after Wentworth had been hurled to the floor. That left a twelfth.

"Sit!" Wentworth croaked at them again. *"Sit!"*

As the men filed to their places about the table, Wentworth lunged at the trailing wires which had connected with the statuette of Buddha. The Dragon-man must be near! His voice… Wentworth came to a halt with an oath of disappointment. The wires simply connected with a regular electrical outlet in the baseboard. He snatched up the Buddha and knew the secret. This statuette was a wired wireless—a device by which it was possible to send messages over the regular electrical circuit of any building. There was no clue here to the Dragon-man!

Wentworth whirled from it to the nine men seated about the table. Buried in their consciousness was the secret of the thing that had happened here tonight. They might even know the intent of the Dragon-man or his identity, since they had been doomed to kill themselves! And Wentworth had the key to make them talk, the voice of the Dragon-man. If only he could work swiftly….

Wentworth sat quietly at the head of the table and looked

over the faces of the nine men before him. He tightened his throat and began to speak in the Dragon voice.

"Report!" he rasped. "Report to the Master. *You* there!"

He leveled his hand at the man nearest to him, stared directly into the glazed unseeing eyes which were so like those of Kirkpatrick. God, what was this horror that threatened the people? What powers did this Dragon-man have that he could reduce intelligent, strong-willed men to slavish automatons willing even to take their own lives at the whispered sound of the Dragon voice!

"We have done your will, master," the man was mumbling. "We have signed over all our wealth, all our holdings to Roderick Hame. He has left us to join you. We have done your will, Master!"

Wentworth whipped to his feet. He had come too late then! The twelfth man had already left to join the Dragon-man. Wait! There was still a way! These men were completely subjected to the will of the Dragon-man! Unless Roderick Hame had some special knowledge which would lead him to the Dragon-man, he must be answering the call of the Dragon-man's will. These other men could do the same. They....

Wentworth seized the shoulder of the man who had spoken. "You are Roderick Hame!" he said rapidly. "You are Roderick Hame and it is the command of the Master that you come to him at once! Understand, Roderick Hame! You will come to the Master at once!"

The man's face worked, as if his muscles fought against paralysis. His tongue moved dryly in his mouth. "Roderick Hame," he muttered. "I am Roderick Hame!" He lurched to his feet, prostrated himself on the floor, and thrice pounded his forehead there. "Master, I come!"

He plodded, stiff-legged, mechanically, toward the door... and a burst of green light blazed into the room from the darkness outside! Wentworth wrenched his head that way and his eyes were dazzled by the rocket glare of the signal Jackson had fired. The police were at hand then! Even as he gazed, a white rocket burst beside the green one. Extreme danger! Wentworth swore harshly. He had the key to the entire mystery in his hand. This man would lead him to the Dragon-man... and the police had ringed the building to trap him!

Wentworth sprang to the window and peered out into the canyon far below. The wind whined coldly about him, seemed to lift to his ears the voices of the hundred or more men in police blue who crowded the streets beneath; a cry that was only too terribly familiar in the midst of the battles that the years had brought:

"Death! Death to the Spider!"

CHAPTER 5
THE GOLDEN DRAGON
THRONE

NITA VAN SLOAN had no time for fright when she felt the floor open beneath her feet in the underground passageway of Chinatown—though there flashed through her brain the instant realization that this was some trap sprung by the Dragon-man. Her eyes caught a brief final glimpse of Richard Wentworth's face, smiling tautly back at her in reassurance... and then darkness.

Ram Singh's great furious shout rang out curiously, beaten back by the close-pressing walls. It swelled enormously as the trapdoor flicked back into place over their heads and then Nita's instinctively flexed legs took the shock of landing. The force of the fall hurled her to the ground, but she picked herself up instantly, turned to reassure Ram Singh. The words never passed her lips.

In the darkness about her there was furious movement, the sharp panting exhalations of fighting men. Before Nita could bring her gun to bear in the pitch blackness, rough hands seized on her. A cloth was slapped tightly across her mouth and she was picked up and borne away, still struggling, but with what futility the iron grip of her captors soon proved. She relaxed then and waited. Dick would soon rip a way through that trapdoor. With such a deliverer intent on her rescue, she could afford to wait!

The men who carried her ran in utter silence save for the slap-slap of bare feet upon the earthen floors and an occasional grunted monosyllable which, though she had a smattering of several Chinese dialects, told her nothing at all. The men seemed to see perfectly in the darkness or they knew the way they traveled with the ease of long familiarity. Abruptly, they burst out into the light and came to an instant halt.

She felt herself deposited on her knees and rough hands pressed her down until her forehead rested on the floor. For a wild moment, Nita fought against them, for she was crouched in the traditional posture of Chinese execution! In imagination, she could see a sharp up-raised sword....

The hands released her, and Nita struggled to her feet, gazed blankly around her. Whatever men had borne her to this spot had vanished in an instant. She stood alone in the middle of a silk-draped hall that was a throne-room. Its illumination had seemed brilliant at first, in contrast to the darkness through which she had been carried. But now she was there the only light came from great tripods which sent flickers of red flame, redolent of incense, toward the silk-swathed ceiling.

Fear was cold within Nita now, but she resisted its sharp probings. Well she knew that her freedom was only apparent. Undoubtedly, those silken wall coverings concealed doorways which might lead to escape, but every one of them would be doubly and triply guarded. And there were eyes watching her, cynically-amused eyes of the East, gazing on a captive white woman. Nita's head came up proudly.

A slight smile came to her lips. From a pocket of her evening cloak, she drew out her cigarette case and, crossing to one of the flaming tripods, used its perfumed fire to light her cigarette. Afterward she strolled about the hall, making her every movement casual by intensest effort.

Nita's mind was racing at white heat. She did not know whether her capture had been deliberate or whether it was an accident that the trap had been sprung when she stood upon it. Ram Singh undoubtedly had been plunged into the pit with her, but where the brave fellow was now she had no idea. If her capture had been deliberate, Nita returned to her original thought, then undoubtedly she was to be used as bait to draw Wentworth into a trap—or as hostage to prevent the Spider from battling against the Dragon-man. A slight, mocking smile touched Nita's lips. If they thought by that means to stop the Spider, they had underestimated him badly!

Light was slowly increasing at the far end of the hall, Nita realized. She turned that way deliberately, smoking, watching for what would be revealed—that slight smile still lingering on her lips. Nita's fears were as great as any woman's would have been; but she had a pride that upheld her in any adversity, the pride of a woman beloved by a great and courageous man. No matter what terror writhed within her, her captors would never know it! SHE COULD see faintly now what had hidden in the darkness before, what she had guessed must be here since she had been forced into a kowtow on entrance. It was a throne. But she was unprepared for the full vision, for the creature that occupied the elevated seat of majesty. At first glance, she had thought that the man was a living representation of Buddha, but the brighter lights brought a shudder of horror that she could scarcely control. For instead of the placid, contemplative and dignified face of the Gautama, she beheld, beneath the jewel-glittering cap—*a human skull!*

Though she recognized that this was but mummery intended to horrify, the reproduction of moldering, age-browned bone, the blank stare of those empty sockets, was so realistic that Nita felt a paralyzing cold over her body. Instinctively, she drew the ermine cloak closer.

She saw that the throne on which this monster sat was made

in the likeness of a huge orchid, blood red and horribly sinister with its suggestion of awful death; that it was flanked on each side by spikes of the hideous flower. With a fascination she could not resist, Nita's eyes probed the shadows about the base of those

The blow of the whip bit into her
shoulder, drove Nita to her knees!

lethal plants and a scream rose unbidden to her throat. Those
gruesome parasites were rooted in… human flesh!

Anger was Nita's immediate reaction, fury against a creature
who could destroy human beings in so vile a way and for the
sole end that his throne should be enshrined in the awful flower.
If she had had a gun… The figure on the throne was speaking,

and its voice came out in the eerie hissing intonation of him who they had christened, in their minds, the Dragon-man….

She listened.

"You have courage, my dear," it said, and the broken-toothed jaw of the skull face worked in an exact reproduction of mouth movements for the words. "A truly rare quality in woman. I may reward that quality, graceful white one, with a place of honor in the imperial harem…."

Somehow, while her flesh crawled with horror, Nita mustered a laugh. It was forced at first, but it came out presently, full and free and scornful. "You!" she mocked. "You… *thing!*"

The impassive skull regarded her, but she felt the impact of anger as if it were a physical thing, and one of the figure's hands moved. Instantly, sound came into the hall—sound which Nita realized was relayed by some sort of loud-speaker hookup. She heard horrid strangling gasps, and the paroxysms of men choking to death terribly!

"The police who sought to help you," came the Dragon voice. "One of those you hear dying is your foolish lover who thought he could wrest from the Dragon that which he desired!"

The awful sounds continued, and then suddenly Nita threw back her head in gay laughter, for she heard Wentworth's voice. It was strained, hoarse, but it was living. "Out of here!" he cried. "Out, I say. Further search will only mean… further deaths!"

The switch was closed and the sound stopped as abruptly as it began, but Nita's courage was high. So long as Dick lived….

"You have been abandoned by your lover!" the Dragon voice

came metallically, mockingly. "Your brave lover who dares not face the fear of death for you!"

Nita let that pass without answer. She knew a faintness that she strove desperately to conceal. Wentworth had done what was possible now to rescue her, and the effort had failed. He would seek other ways while he strove to crush the Dragon-man. But for the present... her own strength must suffice. She had long ago crushed out her first cigarette. Almost languidly, she proceeded to light another from a tripod.

"Richard Wentworth's courage," she said quietly, "is scarcely open to challenge by such a thing as you, fighting in the darkness with coward's weapons. You boast a little too soon, I'm afraid."

"*I boast?*" The anger was unmistakable in the voice now. Almost, Nita thought that she could see the fiery glitter of bitter eyes in the empty sockets of the skull-face. "I, who soon shall be master of the world!"

Nita saw her advantage and seized upon it. She was utterly confident that Dick would rescue her, and meantime there was work she could do here. She could goad this creature into disclosure of his plans. It would help Dick to defeat the Dragon-man and his vile conspiracy. Nita's left hand knotted into a small white fist at her side. Of course it would help. Dick would come for her soon. He... he *had* to come. For an instant, Nita struggled with her fears there, while her pale, proudly aristocratic face was lifted arrogantly. She triumphed over herself, and achieved a careless laugh.

"Many men have boasted of conquering the world," she said

in scorn, "but they did not hide behind such childish masks as that."

The Dragon Voice echoed her laughter, but with a hissing intonation that was horrible in its reptilian suggestion. "Do you think to trap me into revealing myself by any such foolish trickery as that?" it mocked. "No, no. Great men often must begin small. Already, I have mastered the police and all China serves me. When I have struck a few more blows, taken control of the great brains of your country, I shall reveal myself. That will be time enough."

"Coward's blows!" Nita flung at him. "The murder of a poor little Chinese girl whose only sin was piety and loyalty! The murder of an old feeble man in his bed!"

THE FIGURE on the throne leaned forward and Nita saw the fingers of the right hand touch a knife hilt half-hidden in the draperies. Nita faced the throne defiantly, head lifted, arms rigidly at her sides, as if she offered her life, too—as if she could expect no more than slaughter at the hands of such a creature....

"Strike!" she urged him, low-voiced, red lips twisted in bitterness. "It will suit your particular style of conquest!"

"Be careful!" the Dragon Voice warned. "Be careful, woman, lest you goad me too far. I will not tolerate such terms! Coward's blows! Listen. Tonight, I shall seize two score men whose brains have contrived the greatest inventions of the ages. Electrical men. Experts in explosives and machines of war! They shall be my slaves! Within a few hours, too, I shall loot the treasury of the United States government itself! Are these coward's goals? And the very people whom I conquer shall fall down and worship me, the Giver of Dreams!"

Nita somehow twisted her face into a semblance of admiration. His last phrase puzzled her, but that could wait until she learned more. "Those are a man's plans!" she cried. "Tell me, how...."

If a skull could smile, that face, horrible beneath the jeweled cap of Buddha, contrived a smile. The laughter came hissingly. "No, woman. You have learned enough. Perhaps, when you have entered my harem...."

Nita flung back her head and laughed. It was laughter that burst beyond the iron control of her will, tinged with hysteria. She gasped with it, was shaken in every fiber of her being. "Your harem, fool?" she cried. "I will kill myself first! Do you think that any woman who held the love of such a man as Richard Wentworth could bear to look on such a thing as you. You... you imitation of a beast. You...."

Nita did not see the signal, but a hand abruptly slapped across her mouth, sent her reeling backward. Almost she fell, but caught her balance. Red stains sprang out upon her cheeks. It was a coolie who had struck her, a coolie naked to the waist, chest bulging with muscles. About his loins was a red sash and, thrust through it, the great executioner's sword! Nita drew herself up.

"It is enough!" The Dragon Voice was cold with fury. "You shall die, but not pleasantly. When we have the time to give to such a delicate process, you shall die, lingeringly. Oh, I promise you, not too quickly! And the time shall come soon. Take her away!"

The blow of a whip bit into her shoulder, drove Nita to her knees. She bit back a moan of agony, set her white teeth in the full redness of her lower lip. Another blow scourged her to her feet, and the curtains ahead were whipped apart for her passage. Nita broke into a stumbling run and always the lash reached out to lay its agonizing thong across her back. Somewhere presently she sagged to her knees and knew that the whip no longer tortured her; knew that an iron door had swung heavily shut to hold her prisoner... a prisoner of the torturous death that the Dragon-man would presently allot.

Nita's lips parted in a sob that was half a prayer. "Dick!" she whispered. "Oh, Dick...."

It was at that same instant that, high in the Crofts building, Wentworth beheld Jackson's signals of danger and, peering from the window, saw that it was surrounded by hordes of police intent on capturing and finishing, once and for all, the mockeries of the Spider. Had Nita known that she must have given way utterly to despair. But with her, as with Wentworth, while life lasted, there would be hope and a determination to triumph over difficulties.

HOW LONG she lay there, swooning from pain, Nita did not know. Presently, when her reviving strength enabled her to stand, to peer about the confines of her prison cell, she heard once more the shuffle of bare feet in the corridor. Her captors had come to bring her before the Dragon throne for the "delicate death" the skull-faced monster had promised! For one instant,

Nita lifted her face toward the heavens that, somewhere above, must still arch the city in whose depths she was confined.

"Dick!" she whispered. "Dick, come soon, or..." She braced her shoulders, shook off fear like a cloak. If Dick did not come, they would meet some day in some... other world. With bitter effort, Nita prepared herself for the eventuality of death and the indignity of the torture which she knew awaited her.

She thought of her love and, when the door opened, it found her with a smile on her lips, ready.

Her eyes narrowed then at the sight of those who had come for her. There were four of the muscular coolies, but in their midst stood another woman with the blue-black hair of the Orient, with vividly red lips prominent in a pallor-stricken face. In her hair, seeming to focus all the vitality of the woman's suavely rounded figure, she wore the red orchid of death! Nita knew her then, recognized her as one whom the Chinese had called the Blood Orchid... just before little Hwang-yo had died with that loathsome flower bursting through the girl flesh of her breast!

The orchid woman smiled with a rich slow movement of that too red mouth. "I owe you some thanks, woman," she said to Nita, her voice slurred into the sing-song accents of the East. "The Master is too prone to admire your kind, and your rough tongue has saved me from your... competition. So, if I can, I shall... shorten your sufferings. Come!"

Nita made no answer to the woman but she knew a shrinking of her flesh as she stepped past her to a place among the squared guard of half-naked coolies. She saw a whip at the belt of one of the men, and her teeth caught at her lip in a swift, instinctive dread. Resolutely, she fought down the terror. If she must die in agony, she would show them how the love of the Spider could support her! She even permitted herself to smile upon the Orchid Woman.

"You are kind," she said flatly. "But what has to be borne, I can bear!"

Nita saw admiration shine in the woman's sloe-black eyes, but there was no answer and the slow, yet all too rapid, march along the corridors to the throne-room and torture was begun. Nita tried to put the dread of what lay ahead from her mind, forced her thoughts to other things. Ram Singh! What had become of him? Was she wrong in thinking that he had plunged into the trap with her? For a moment, a little gleam of hope warmed in her breast, but she resolutely forced it down. If the valiant Sikh had fallen, he, too, had been captured. Perhaps, he would be there to die beside her.

A moment later, she stepped through into the throne room and saw her fears confirmed. Already, Ram Singh was stretched upon a vertical torture rack. His muscle-corded arms and legs were stretched to the four corners of the frame and she saw upon his body the marks of torture already begun. But, amid the thick curling beard, his lips moved to flash his white teeth in a smile.

"*Salaam, missie sahib!*" he cried in his deep, resonant voice. "These pigs do not permit that thy servant greet thee as is meet!"

"*Wah!* For shame!" Nita answered him, smiling. "Can pigs prevent a man from his duty? These are no pigs, but crawling turtles."

Nita had not yet looked at the throne, but she heard a hiss of rage at this greatest of insults to a Chinese and rough hands forced her to her knees and knocked her forehead upon the floor. Her hands were wrenched behind her back and a rope bit into the soft flesh of her wrists. Suddenly, there was intolerable strain upon them and Nita felt herself being hoisted upward by that bond. Her shoulders were wrenched almost to the breaking point. Her feet left the floor... Nita's breath was driven from her lungs by the pain. She formed the breath into a word.

"Turtles!" she whispered. *"Turtles...."*

Words came to her ears dimly, a Chinese attempting to pronounce an English name, and abruptly the pressure on her arms was relaxed. She found herself dizzily on her feet and, through the haze that agony laid upon her brain, realized that the Dragon Voice was speaking to her.

"Your lover, Wentworth," it said sibilantly, "is arriving just in time to see you die. He is trying to enter by the stupid trick of pretending to be Roderick Hame, who already has arrived. How he contrived to find our retreat..." The voice interrupted itself. "No matter. Before you die, I wish you to see your lover walk into the trap which I have contrived!"

Even as he spoke, Nita heard a man scream somewhere in the distance, muffled by the underground passageways through which the voice had come; scream with the agony of a man come suddenly and unaware upon awful death. And mingled with that cry was the mocking laughter of the skull-faced thing on the throne!

That scream was broken across by the crashing thunder of a

gunshot! One of the half-naked coolies thunder-bolted back-ward through the silken hangings that draped the wall and, through the opening that had been revealed sprang a figure in a black swirling cape—a hunched figure with guns in its fists! From the lips of the intruder came flat, mocking, sinister laugh-ter, the laughter of the Spider!

"Die, Dragon!" he cried, and the twin guns swiveled and spat hot lead toward the squat and awful figure on the throne of the Blood Orchid!

CHAPTER 6
HELL'S HURRICANE!

SWIFT AS had been Wentworth's attack upon the murderous mock-idol upon the throne, one other had been swifter. In the split-second before he had fired, the orchid woman had darted through the silken hangings on the wall. Even as the guns leaped in Wentworth's hands and sped their deadly lead, the entire throne plunged downward through the floor! The golden silks behind the throne jerked with the impact of Wentworth's bullets and showed how true his aim had been… but it was too late!

A cry sprang from Wentworth lips. In two long strides, he was beside the already closed trapdoor through which the throne had dropped—was pumping bullets down upon it. They tore the wood… and ricocheted from the steel which lay under it! That moment of defeat might have spelled disaster to a lesser man than Richard Wentworth, but his mind was not clouded by futile anger. As quickly as he understood the nature of the trick, Wentworth sprang into action again. Not in pursuit or in vain racing through dark corridors. Instead, he pivoted where he stood, in a quick leap reached the side of the Chinese coolie guard he had killed, and wrested the mighty sword from its sash scabbard.

A whistling slash severed the rope that a moment before had tortured Nita, and she felt the bonds loosen on her wrists. That cut was delivered in passing, as the Spider leaped toward Ram Singh. The blade glittered in a short arc, the slash of a master swordsman that would not waver a hair's breadth from its sure mark. Ram Singh's right arm snapped free of its prisoning bond and an instant later, his left hand followed suit.

Wentworth thrust the hilt into the Sikh's eager grip and, instantly, the Spider's guns were speaking. Within less than two seconds after he had made his vain attempt to rid the world of the monster criminal, he had freed his two companions. And his swift bullets were crashing out the lights which made them so perfect a target for the enemies that surrounded them!

So quickly had Wentworth reformed his plan of battle that, before a counter-attack could be launched, he had Nita and Ram Singh beside him and was stealing back along the corridor by which he had entered. Nita longed to throw herself into his arms, but that, like their love, must ever wait upon the brief moments of safety in the Spider's violent life.

"*Wah, sahib!*" growled Ram Singh. "Shall we run from these cowardly pigs? There are no more than a score of them, and thou and I, mighty warriors...."

Wentworth's laughter was soft. "Silence, thou lion! The

Master is hiding behind a thousand devil's traps by this time. Why should a lion claw mice, while the greater game escapes?"

The Sikh growled his assent and Nita moved closer to Wentworth. "I have no weapon," she whispered, in a voice she struggled to make firm. She had been so close to death, and now Dick was with her. Her Dick... The cold touch of steel filled her hand and she gripped the small automatic.

"This way," Wentworth whispered. "We are almost directly under the Municipal Office Building. There is no time to be lost. That clever devil will be closing all the exits, and...."

Wentworth cut his words short then for a new sound began to roll through the corridor they followed—the whine of a rising wind!

Wentworth stopped short, listening. It was an incredible sound to hear far beneath the surface of the earth, but he could not be mistaken. There was the hissing moan of a storm and, already, its cold breath was beginning to pluck at the cape that swung from his shoulders.

"It's some trap," Wentworth whispered. "Hurry!"

He pushed forward into the thrust of the wind, drawing Nita and Ram Singh with him. They must go forward. Behind them lay death, lurking. The blast had increased incredibly in that short while. Wentworth found himself leaning far forward to maintain his balance. His breath was driven back into his lungs so that in order to breathe he was compelled to muffle his nostrils in the crook of his arm. He could feel Nita's hands, clinging desperately, and flung an arm about her, though he still gripped his guns. Of what use were guns in such a fury as this?

68

He lifted a foot to take another step forward and hurriedly planted it on the ground again as he felt the wind thrust him backward a half-step. He realized grimly that the gale was still increasing! They were trapped in a wind-tunnel whose peak velocity no man could guess, but he knew that in the testing laboratories of airplane factories, such enclosures could house a hurricane. Long before this force of violent air reached any such peak, they would be torn from their footing, tumbled down this corridor... to such a fate as only the ingenuity of their monster foe could devise!

WENTWORTH'S CAPE was billowing straight out from his shoulders and, with a quick hand, he freed it from him, heard it flap and flutter off into the darkness behind them. Even lifting his arm was an effort now. It was like moving against a solid rushing wall of water. Wentworth's feet began to slip....

"Down!" he cried, and the wind whipped his voice instantly from his lips. "Down on your faces for your lives!"

He had to fight to reach the earth, to drag Nita down beside him. His fingers clawed for a hold on a floor that was smooth as glass. Even that was of no avail. With a sense of helpless, rising horror, he realized that they were beginning to slide backward along the corridor! His hat had long since been whipped from his head, and the lank wig which the Spider wore. The wind strained at his clothing like titan's hands. Laboriously, Wentworth thrust an automatic into its holster and dragged out a small powerful flashlight which he always carried. He twisted his head and threw its beam back along the corridor behind

• NITA VAN SLOAN •

them, and a cry rose to his lips—a cry he himself could scarcely hear above the wolf howl of the wind.

A wall of steel was behind them—a wall which allowed space around its edges for the winds to push past, but no more. And needling out from that steel wall was a forest of yard-long lances! That horrible man-made porcupine wall already had claimed one victim. Apparently, one of the Chinese had been pursuing them, knife in hand, when the wind trap had been turned loose

70

upon the tunnel. Unprepared, or nearer to that fearful wall, he had been hurled upon the spikes and instantly pierced through and through in a dozen places!

In that single swift glimpse of the hell behind them, Wentworth also spotted Ram Singh. The great Sikh, head bowed into the storm, had braced his hands against opposite sides of the walls and, with bulging muscles, held himself by main force against the storm. The fragmentary clothing left him by the Chinese torturers was already shredding. Tags of it cracked like tiny whip lashes in the torrent of air. His beard was parted, torn, and white, locked teeth between shrinking lips showed the strain of his effort. Even as Wentworth looked, the gale scooped Ram Singh's turban from his head and hurled it like a projectile against the wall, impaled it there.

"The sword!" Wentworth cried. "The sword, Ram Singh. Drive it into the wall!"

The Sikh's dark eyes were rolling with fatigue. He stared at Wentworth through a long moment before the words penetrated and, in that moment, Wentworth once more began to

slide along the glassy floor, propelled helplessly. He made a swift change, braced his shoulders against one wall and straightened his legs against the other, and slid almost ten feet in the process. He was within a foot of the straining bronze columns of Ram Singh's legs now. Nita, his arm about her body, lay with her feet toward those spikes. Her hair was peeled back from her forehead and made her eyes seem enormous. She was clinging with both arms, and she bowed her head into his chest. He could feel her shuddering efforts to breathe. Fumbling, one-handed, Wentworth freed his belt.

"Catch the end, Ram Singh!" he cried. "Hold it while you drive the sword into the wall! I can't hold out much longer!"

He held the belt aloft, and the wind flicked its end against Ram Singh's chest. The Sikh's massive head bowed. Slowly, slowly, he drew a leg forward and braced it afresh. He grabbed at the belt and his feet were swept out from under him. His lips tore open in what Wentworth knew was his war shout, but no sound of it reached Wentworth's ears. At the wrench upon the belt, Wentworth was rolled half-over and the gale seized on him with a thousand powerful hands, began to roll him toward destruction.

When he stopped himself, he was face-down, his chest bearing Nita's shoulders to earth. But he still held the belt. By the jerks upon it, he knew that Ram Singh was struggling to carry out the orders.

The flashlight had been hurled against the steel wall and its crazy, tilted light spilled grotesque shadows. With wavering senses, Wentworth thought that it was strange that even shadows could stand against this hurricane! His breath came in jerking rasps….

An enormous while seemed to roar past and then, firm under his shoulder, he felt Ram Singh's braced leg taking the strain off his own muscles. Feebly, with incredible effort, he turned his head. The sword was buried a foot deep in the wall and Ram Singh, back pressed to the same wall, had taken the flat of the blade under his arm as a brace.

His eyes were open wide, his teeth still clenched with enormous effort—but he was rock-steady.

SOME SEMBLANCE of rational thought was beginning to return to Wentworth. The storm of wind had reached its peak, but knew no cessation. Amid its tumult, Wentworth forced himself to seek a way out. In wind tunnels, these titanic drafts were caused by great electrically turned turbines, whirling at incredible speeds.

At the thought, hope began to pour its warming stream through him. The turbine must be squarely across this passage, and the drive would be at its middle. If he could seek out the motor with bullets, or even puncture the blades, it would disrupt, perhaps wreck the machine, as when a metal propeller on an airplane was torn. The very velocity of the blades would enlarge the opening, throw it off balance….

Laboriously, Wentworth dragged out his holstered automatic and pointed its muzzle into the wind. He found himself wondering hysterically if a bullet could bore into that hurricane wall. Something like laughter pumped at his chest; the gale gagged him. He began to shoot….

Sometime in the hour-long minutes that followed, punctuated by the slamming of his heavy guns, the drawn-out howl of the hurricane changed. A thin and angry note broke its deep diapason; rose to a high-pitched snarl. Frantically, Wentworth increased his fire. The shriek of tortured machinery became an unbearable scream; there was a shattering clatter, a muffled explosion—and silence that fell like a blow. With the sudden relaxation of the wind's force Ram Singh pitched across Wentworth's body like a falling tree.

For seconds they lay, almost incapable of realizing that the wind had ceased. Then Wentworth dragged himself to his feet like an aged and decrepit man. His chest ached and there were tremors in all his muscles. Laboriously, Wentworth lifted Nita.

"Quickly," Wentworth urged, and his voice made a startling shout along the corridor. "Quickly, before the hordes are upon us!"

He turned to Ram Singh and found the Sikh adjusting his rescued turban with shaking hands. "Thy strength saved us, my warrior!" he said.

"*Wah!*" Ram Singh's grunt was eloquent of disgust. "I am like a woman for weakness, master." He gripped the hilt of the sword and wrenched it from its socket between the bricks of the wall. Then he stumbled into a leap, the mighty blade ready in his fist. "They are cowards, these turtles who fight with the winds of heaven."

Wentworth had loaded the last charges into his automatics and he held them ready as they fumbled on through the tunnels to an exit in a dilapidated office building's basement. Once more, the Chinese had sprung their deadly trap and fled to other hiding places—or had they sped to fresh tasks of horror? Jackson was at his post with the Daimler and, gratefully, Wentworth relaxed against the cushions. His smile as he turned to Nita was wry.

"It hasn't been a very pleasant evening out dear," he said dryly.

Nita's lips were stiff as they curved in an answering smile. "I learned a lot from the Dragon-man," she said slowly. "When I have got a little strength back... I must look a fright." Her trembling hands touched her wind-torn hair.

Wentworth drew her head to his shoulder, his arm fiercely about her while his eyes probed the darkness of the night. He saw that Jackson was driving along illy lighted side streets, weaving a devious way uptown, and his eyes tightened as he picked up the speaking-tube and threw a quick question.

"Police broadcast, sir," Jackson reported crisply. "Orders out for your arrest on suspicion. And you're in disguise."

Wentworth's hand reached upward to his face. The wind had left little of his disguise, but he removed the remnants swiftly.

He was ready.

Nita thrust herself erect, "What happened to those twelve men Fu-Chang said were in danger, and what did he mean by saying the police department was already mastered?"

Wentworth's face grew grim as he swiftly narrated the things that had happened in Kirkpatrick's office and in the Crofts building. "Jackson's signal gave me plenty of time to escape the police," he said quietly. "I disguised myself as one of the board of directors and imitated their movements. Afterward, when we were being rushed to a hospital, I abducted one of the men and persuaded him, by using the Dragon's voice, that he was Roderick Hame. He led me directly to the Dragon's hideout, poor fellow. They killed him."

Wentworth saw bewilderment and a trace of fear in Nita's face. "He *led* you," she said, "but how could his belief that he was Roderick Hame take you to the Dragon-man?"

Wentworth shook his head and his lips tightened. "There are occult things in the East which, perhaps, we shall never penetrate," he said. "I have before this run into the 'extension of will' as I believe they call it. Apparently, the Dragon-man was calling Roderick Hame, whom he had previously hypnotized and drugged, to his hideout. This other man, also hypnotized, could receive that call… I do not know how. I only know that every hour brings fresh dread to me—and fresh disasters to the people. He reaped millions by tonight's coup in seizing the property of the Chinamerc company. I'll have Kirk…."

Wentworth's voice died as he remembered in what state he had left Kirkpatrick. Police facilities might succeed in tracing the transfer of that stock, but probably Roderick Hame would continue to draw the wealth and pay it over on demand….

Nita gripped his arm and he turned to find her eyes wide and frightened. "So many things have happened, Dick," she whispered. "They almost drove from my mind the things I found out. This Dragon-man aims at world conquest!" Rapidly then, she told him what she had learned, of the Dragon-man's boast that he would seize the great inventive brains of the nation in munitions and electrical fields.

Wentworth swore softly and fresh anxiety drove the fatigue from his body. "I doubt that he's well-organized yet outside of this state," he said. "Undoubtedly, he means to raid the big laboratories at Albany and Pittsboro. Jackson, find me a telephone that I can use without being spotted! As for looting the treasury of the United States, that is ridiculous, with its powerful defenses. Unless... unless he means to rob some of the shipments that are carrying silver and gold to the nation's new repositories! Even so, it seems unbelievable."

Jackson spun the heavy Daimler around a corner and a wild-driving car narrowly missed charging into them. It wove its erratic way on down the street and Wentworth gazed after it with heavily-frowning brows.

"The Dragon-man said something else, Dick," Nita told him swiftly. "He said that when he came as a conqueror, the country would welcome him as the 'Giver of Dreams.' I can't guess what he meant."

Wentworth was still frowning as he looked at her. "The Chinese ideograph for that phrase—"he sketched rapidly on the palm of his hand—"is the same as that which means poppy—the opium poppy. I don't quite understand...."

HE STOPPED abruptly as Jackson jammed on brakes in an emergency halt. A stream of young people was straggling across the street, laughing and singing. They seemed completely unaware of the heavy car which had so narrowly missed running them down. A boy and girl stopped beneath a street light, kissing fervently.

"The town's full of drunks tonight," Nita said resignedly.

Wentworth stared at the group of youths and did not answer. "Wait, Jackson!" he ordered shortly and, springing to the pavement, stalked after the shambling crowd. He overtook one of the boys and whirled him about, face to the light, peered into his dark, expanded eyes. Wentworth swore in harsh anger.

"Where did you get it?" he demanded "Speak up!" The boy grinned foolishly. "Swell dinner," he mumbled. "Perfectly swell. What do you mean. Where did we get *what?*"

"The opium!" Wentworth shook him slightly.

The boy's face flushed indignantly. "You're nuts!" he said violently. "Absolute nuts! Wouldn't use opium. Just had a little fun at the Red Dragon…" He wrenched free and went shuffling off up the street, moving like one in a dream, which indeed he was—a boy in the roseate clouds of an opium dream!

Wentworth swore harshly as he swung back to the car. Youngsters drugged with opium, without their own knowledge! He realized now, and realized terribly what the Dragon-man meant by being hailed as the 'Giver of Dreams!' Well might he boast that the people would welcome him, if he could spread wholesale over the land the demoralizing opium habit. It would take tons of the fearful drug, but to a man powerful in the only nation in the world where the poppy was grown without regulation, that would offer no great obstacle if he could smuggle it into the country.

Despair seized Wentworth as he flung himself against the cushions and ordered Jackson to drive on. There was so little he could do! Tip off the narcotic division, of course, and have them tighten up their search for the drug—but the chances were that the Dragon-man already had his supplies in the country. He had certainly smuggled himself and his followers in... With choked voice, he told Nita.

"The fiend's plans are unfolding," he said harshly. "God knows what horror we'll discover next. If he succeeds in abducting those scientists, he has the means to make them his slaves. Think what it would mean to have the greatest scientific brains of the country working for a criminal! And the police force is crippled with Kirkpatrick disabled. I hope Doctor Ridley...."

He broke off as Jackson halted the car in a dark side street where there was a small confectionery shop with the blue sign of a telephone booth outside. Wentworth sprang from the car, stopped tensely as he spotted the blue uniform and brass buttons of a policeman... but only for a moment. The cop was propped up against a wall and his lolling head and slouched posture told Wentworth more plainly than any words that here was another who this night had tasted the dreams of the poppy!

Wentworth's face was drawn and taut as he slid into the telephone booth and put through a call to an Albany friend who worked in the electrical laboratories there. He waited tensely through seeming hours until a sleepy voice, a woman's voice, answered the phone. Wentworth identified himself rapidly.

"Is John Haskins there?" he asked. "It is terribly urgent."

The woman's voice quickened, "I'm sorry, he's not, Mr. Wentworth. There was an emergency meeting called at the laboratories tonight. Is there any message?"

Wentworth hesitated, but what could he say? Haskins and the other men at the laboratories would laugh at any warning he could give thus secondhand over the phone. It would take much more than that to send them to the police, to break up their session....

What could he do?

Wentworth was suddenly certain that the meeting was a ruse to draw the men together in one place so that the Dragon-man could strike! God, he must make the effort, fore-doomed though he knew it to be. Rapidly, he warned the woman, then rang off on her promise to do all she could. He could hear the incredulity and suspicion in her voice.

Wentworth next tried to raise the laboratory itself, but there was no answer, only the operator's voice reporting, "The line seems to be out of order!" If Wentworth had needed confirmation of his fears, he had it now! The operator's report could only mean that... the wires were cut! He must race to Albany himself and hope against hope that he could arrive in time! Yet there was some reason for hope. At least he knew where next the Dragon-man would strike. He might perhaps form contact there with the damnable yellow scourge and hope to track him down and kill him! There was no other way in which he could stop this series of outrages; to check the threatened demoralization of the people with drugs.

WENTWORTH RAN back to the car, sent it racing toward his home. Undoubtedly, the police would be on the lookout for him there, but he had secret means of ingress that he used only in extreme emergency. He directed Jackson toward the entrance now, relayed his discoveries to Nita.

"You must keep trying by telephone, Nita," he said tensely.

"Try to make those fools realize the danger. Call the police… Get hold of Ridley and see if he has succeeded in reviving Kirkpatrick. They might listen to him, up there in Albany, and in Pittsboro. Perhaps, some government official…."

"I'll take care of it, Dick," Nita said quietly, while her hand crept into his. "Don't worry…" The weakness of her words stopped her.

Not worry when the city seemed to be disintegrating before their very eyes? She tried to convey her sympathy and understanding through the touch of their hands. There was so little, so very little that she could do… and Dick was going into grave danger again. Nita did not need to be told that, and she would not hold him back if she could. Only, it was hard to lose him when so recently death had nearly torn them apart!

"I'll… do my best," she said again, slowly, fighting the grief from her voice.

Wentworth heard and understood, drew her tenderly into his arms while his wide open eyes stared blindly at the streets through which they raced. What horror lay ahead of the city's people God alone knew, but the past few hours had shown plenty! He felt an overweening sense of helplessness that was strange to the Spider. Each feeble blow he had struck against the enemy had been returned a hundred-fold, and he had barely managed to fight off death itself… Something very like a groan forced itself out between his compressed lips. God help his poor suffering country now; and God help the scientists in Albany if they failed to heed his warning….

CHAPTER 7
SLAVES OF THE DRAGON

FROM VARIOUS places around Albany, some score or more of automobiles converged on the huge Universal Laboratories. Some were driven by chauffeurs; some contained lone men, but one and all they carried scientists who wore puzzled frowns. It was a strange thing in these peaceful days to receive a night summons to a conference at the laboratories, a call that brooked no delay. None of the men phoned to verify the orders, but if any had, it would not have aroused suspicion. The phone wires were not cut until the last man had entered the warmly lighted, waiting laboratories.

It was a fine, modern building, constructed in accordance with all the latest principles of science, as befitted one of the world's largest electrical laboratories. It had air conditioning among other things, and the plant was running at full strength when the men hurried in to wait for their president who had summoned them—whom they *thought* had summoned them....

It is probable that not even the watchmen noticed two men who stole away into the shadows a few moments after that last arrival. But if anyone did see, it aroused no suspicion. Why should it when so many men had gone openly into the main administrative building? The gate watchman paced his narrow beat before the cubicle set up there for him, and puffed at a pipe. Now and then he glanced upward at the star-spangled sky. It was clear, deep blue, and though gazing at it may have given the watchman some little pleasure, it would not help the twenty-five scientists inside. The danger would *not* come from the sky....

Minutes dragged, became a half hour, an hour finally, while the men still waited. Under less extraordinary circumstances, some would have gone home, probably. None did. It was true that one of the older men finally went to the telephone to call the home of the president and found the line out of order, but he only shrugged in annoyance, unsuspicious.

Scientists often are not practical men, and Otto Himmler was not. He was a stoop-shouldered fellow with a shock of gray-shot hair and mild blinking eyes behind his thick spectacles. He was anxious to get back home to bed, that was all. These cold days, he felt his age a little more and sleep was good to an overactive brain. He coughed a little and worried about the possibility that he might contract a cold. It never occurred to him that there might be something... *irritating* in the warm circulated air of the building. In this modern age, air conditioning eliminated such things... unless the plant had been tampered with!

John Haskins, the friend whom Wentworth had called in vain, sat with his long legs thrust out before him and sucked moodily at a pipe. Occasionally, he lifted his head in the quick way he had and glanced at the big electric clock, or watched the smoke from his pipe thin and vanish into the louvres of the ventilating system.

Once or twice, he coughed also, and glared irritably at his pipe. He'd been smoking too much again, he supposed. It couldn't be the scientifically humidified air of the plant. Of course not. But he noticed that other men coughed now and again as they plodded about the lavish meeting-room and grumbled at the delay, or gathered in little impromptu circles to mock at one another's theories.

An hour had passed when John Haskins, who had been the first to arrive, rose to his feet and knocked out his pipe with a gesture of finality.

"I'm going home," he announced shortly to the room at large. He stretched and winced at a little catch of pain in his chest and pressed a palm against it experimentally. "You lads can give me the old man's message in the morning."

He stumped toward the door and a cough caught in his throat. It hurt and he was suddenly coughing very hard, painfully. He was seized by a paroxysm and braced an uncertain hand against the wall while it shook him. He lifted puzzled, annoyed eyes when it was over and found himself gazing into Otto Himmler's mild stare.

"You have caught a cold, yes," Himmler nodded gravely. "It is this air conditioning. Stoves are much better."

Haskins was frowning, but managed a weak smile. There was a sharper, constant pain in his chest now. "That's a hell of a senti-ment for a scientist, Otto," he mocked. "We must be modern, and..." A cough stopped him. The pain in his chest was almost unbearable and the coughs came from deep down, tearing, shak-ing his very heart. Other men were looking at Haskins now, crowding toward him.

"What's the matter, old man? Better go to bed. We'll make your excuses. Sounds like pneumonia."

If Wentworth could have heard, he might have told them

what the cough sounded like, but he would have called it by a harsher name. To his ears, it would have sounded like death! The death that had carried off little Hwang-yo!

Haskins tried to get out some words, endeavored to stagger toward the door, and the pain twisted like hot, clawed steel in his vitals. He sagged to the floor and a gasping moan was wrung from him! Some men tried to pick him up, but abruptly one of them stiffened, staring before him with wide-open eyes. His lungs began to pump with coughing. His hands clawed at his chest.

From the men standing about Haskins, a sudden, frightened shout lifted itself. Otto Himmler was pointing with a veined, shaking hand toward Haskins' chest. Something was thrusting up there like the head of a small, green snake, finding its way out through the rents that Haskins' desperate hands had torn in his shirt.

"God!" old Otto gasped. "It looks like a flower—the bud of a flower!"

Even as he spoke, that green snake's head of virulent growth was opening itself, was spreading bright petals the shade of living blood! They had no name for it, but that deadly flower had a name, and the sight of it would have sent any denizen of Chinatown screaming in flight from the room. *The Blood Orchid had flowered again!*

SANE MEN fled shouting from those doomed halls, but most of them never reached the doors. For those who did attain the open air, there was no relief. Their coughs doubled them, writhing, to the earth and, presently, from their still convulsed bodies, the small snake heads of green thrust upward in their awful flowering....

The watchman left off his gazing at the blue skies and ran into the building. That was a mistake, but he would not learn it for an hour or more. And there was something in the sky now for him to see. A racing plane was streaking its crimson exhausts like a shooting star across the night blue, making its frantic dash from New York City. A landing-flare burst into dazzling light and, moments later, the plane dived down and fish-tailed to earth just outside the laboratory fences.

From its cockpit, a figure sprang and sprinted for the gates, turned toward the building—then came to an abrupt halt. At his feet lay the body of Otto Himmler. From between his shoulder blades, the bright vicious flower of the Blood Orchid glowed! The pilot of the plane ripped off his flying helmet with a violent hand and Wentworth's shocked, infuriated face stared toward the gaily lighted building. It was silent, terribly silent—as still as were the half-dozen forms of men that were strewn from where he stood to the very doors of the plant. And those lights, laying their warm, yellow oblongs on the ground, picked out again and again the bright scarlet of the flower of death.

Wentworth stood for a moment with proud shoulders stooped in defeat, but presently his head pulled up and there was a tight, keen look on his face. He forced himself to walk from body to body there on the lawn and inspect each one. They were men he knew by reputation, all of them. No doubt that these were the ones the Dragon-man had marked for his own.

But he had boasted he would enslave them! Could the Drag-on-man then raise the dead?

Wentworth shook the bewilderment, the futile rage over his tardy arrival, from his brain. Let him keep his mind clear for vengeance! Somewhere here, the men of the Dragon or that fiend himself had passed. Somewhere, there must be a clue that the Spider's keen brain could seize upon and analyze. There *had* to be! Such slaughter could not go on.

Wentworth's fists were tightly clenched as he drove himself to continue the slow march from body to body of these pitiful victims of the Dragon-man's greed. Each one bore the scarlet parasite of death, either on breast or back. That flower was an incredible thing—but was it?

Animal parasites, many of them, lived upon animals and drew sustenance from their unwilling hosts. Others burrowed their way into the vitals of men and animals, or were introduced into the body through food, and lived there, often destroying the creature on whom they fed. Why was it so unbelievable that the horrid ingenuity of the East should discover a plant that did the same? Orchids were as purely parasitic as mistletoe. Always, they lived upon other plants—and now one had been found whose spores would instantly sprout and grow in the tropically warm vitals of a human being!

A sudden thought jerked up Wentworth's head. Some para-sites found their way into human bodies through food! But these deadly flowers invariably sprouted from back or chest as if—as if they had taken root in the lungs! Wentworth under-stood terribly how this horror had been contrived. Spores of the

Blood Orchid had been introduced into the air of the laboratory, perhaps through the air conditioning systems from which filters could easily be removed. The scientists, summoned to a meeting which was never to be held, had inhaled those spores... *and died!*

As quickly as the thought seized Wentworth, he raced back to his plane and whipped out the oxygen mask which he used for high-altitude flights. He was running toward the building while he fitted it on. Inside the door, horror stopped him for a moment as he gazed down on the huddled, distorted bodies of more victims. But he drove himself on and found the basement door. Moments later, he was gazing on the confirmation of his swiftly formed theory: the filters *had* been removed from the air conditioning system!

INSTANTLY, WENTWORTH was streaking toward the plane again. The Dragon-man's threat had been leveled also at the munitions experts in Pittsboro. Wentworth knew that Nita had been trying ceaselessly to warn police and government officials there, but without Commissioner Kirkpatrick of the New York Police to support her advice, it was doubtful if they would listen to her. Besides, she could only warn of an attack. He knew how the killers would strike, and how to guard against them! If only he could reach the right people in time!

The phones here were useless—that he already knew—but once let him gain altitude in his plane, its radio equipment would give him instant contact with Pittsboro... Within a few minutes, Wentworth had sent the ship leaping into the air, was soaring high above the Universal Laboratories with their pitiful toll of dead. He forced his voice to calmness as he held the radio mouthpiece close to his lips, swiftly adjusted his transmitter to the police wave band of Pittsboro.

"Calling Pittsboro police," he said rapidly. "Calling Pittsboro police. All cars near the government munitions plant. Rush with all possible speed to laboratory buildings. Warn workers that a gas attack is being made by spies. A gas attack by spies! Police must don gas masks before entering buildings. More details later."

Wentworth's lips were grim as he manipulated his transmitting set to change the wave band, seeking to reach any amateurs who might be listening in. They might believe his story of a gas attack by spies. Defense against such an attempt would be equally effective against the spores of the Blood Orchid. And the same men who might accept the spy-gas theory would laugh him to scorn if he should attempt to tell the terrible truth: "Wear gas masks or a flower will take root in your lungs and kill you!"

Wentworth broadcast to the amateurs a similar warning, asking them to get in touch with the police; tuned back to the police band again. Afterward, with swift fingers, he removed all limitations from his wavelength, broadcast wholesale the familiar and ominous "SOS." Again and again, he repeated his warning, and now he added a new item.

"This is the Spider calling! The Spider calling the Pittsboro police. All agencies relay the message!"

Wentworth's face was tense as he threw that betraying name to the air waves. It was necessary. The police might well ignore an anonymous message from the air, especially one of such startling purport, but when the Spider spoke, men listened! Wentworth was well aware of the risk he ran in such a course. The instant he announced himself, the police of many cities would begin to triangulate his location. The Dragon-man might well be listening, too! Even if they could not hunt him down in the air, every airport in the entire district would be on the lookout for him! But the Spider never hesitated to imperil himself if, by that means, he might thwart the enemies of mankind!

Wentworth was racing full speed toward Pittsboro with his motor howling, wide open. He could not trust the police to heed his warning and, even if it meant his own capture, he was determined to thwart the Dragon-man, to save the scientists who still were threatened—if God should grant that he was not already too late!

The thought had never been far from Wentworth's brain and, when he had sent the last appeal, and had notified the Albany police of the tragedy nearer them, he began to search the air waves with his receiver, seeking for news of success—or failure. It came, all too soon. An excited news broadcaster broke in upon a musical program....

"Ladies and gentlemen, we interrupt this program to bring you a news flash! A few minutes ago, I told you that an incredible warning had come over the air waves from the Spider, telling the police that there would be a gas attack upon the government munitions laboratories near here. Ladies and gentlemen, the Spider was right! According to news just flashed from police headquarters at Pittsboro, the Spider was right. But his warning came too late! More than forty workers, among them many of the government's leading experts, were found dead in the laboratories. There are no explanations, no details yet. I'll be back when there is more news...."

WENTWORTH BIT down the ragged oath that tore at his throat. Too late! Always just too late in his warfare against the Dragon-man! God knew where this contest must end. In swift succession, the Dragon-man had struck every blow of which he had boasted to Nita—every blow save the looting of the treasury of the United States! Even at this moment, the butcher might be preparing for that crime, too!

Wentworth recalled his guess that the Dragon-man meant to assault the shipments of silver and gold bullion being transported to the new treasure vaults at West Point. The details of this work were a carefully guarded government secret, but Wentworth knew that it was in the charge of a port commander of the coast guard, and that trans-shipment would take place over a period of six months, various routes and methods of transport being used.

One thing became increasingly clear to Wentworth as he swung the nose of his plane toward the Hudson River and New York City. If the Dragon-man had boasted to Nita, it must have been because his plans already were fully laid, and because he had advance knowledge of the government plans. But how could Wentworth warn the guards, or know whether the treasure actually was being shipped tonight?

Nita would try to warn the government, of course; to tip off the police. But they hadn't listened to her in Pittsboro, or Albany. How could he hope that they would now?

Wentworth was close to despair, baffled by the rapidity of

the criminals' covert blows, by his own utter inability to come to grips with a tangible foe. This much was certain: if the Dragon-man planned to steal and carry away gold, his men would have to be present at the scene at the time the crime was committed....

Wentworth set his jaw in grim determination and determined upon a night-long patrol of the Hudson River between New York City and West Point. Whatever route was chosen by the gold guards, that was the territory that must be transversed. It was a known fact that the most careful plans had been laid for the transport; that every precaution against possible criminal attack would be taken... Wouldn't that include an airplane patrol also, lest criminals strike from the sky? The longer he thought over this possibility, the more convinced Wentworth became that precisely such a precaution would be taken. It simplified his work. If he ran into an aerial patrol, or was warned off by another airplane, he could be reasonably sure that it was because a gold shipment was underway!

Swiftly, Wentworth sent his plane skimming southward toward New York, flying low so that he could keep a constant lookout, too, for any transport train of armored trucks. It was soon after he flashed past Bear Mountain bridge that a radio voice rasped coldly on his ear and he glanced sharply aloft to see a trio of planes circling against the night sky.

"This district closed to aerial navigation by government order," the man's voice said crisply. "Turn east and pass at a distance of five miles from the river! Acknowledge. Come in."

Wentworth immediately threw in his transmitter. "Richard

Wentworth speaking," he said sharply. "If you are, as I believe, guarding a shipment of gold to West Point, please take warning. I have had advices tonight that an attempt would be made by the same criminals who killed forty men at Pittsboro, to seize the shipment. Gas was used in the Pittsboro attack. Can you make contact with the transport division below? Come in."

"Thanks," the flier acknowledged over the radiophone. "Turn east at once."

Obediently, Wentworth banked sharply to the left and winged eastward to skirt the zone delimited by the aerial guard, but his anxiety did not lift. The flier had sounded too cocksure. Still, he could hardly fail to relay Wentworth's message, if only as a routine matter. Wentworth dug out night glasses and focused them on the roadways that paralleled the river at his point and presently made out a close-spaced line of headlights crawling up a steep grade. Trucks, they certainly were, and none swung out of line or attempted to pass one another. Moreover, the road was clear of all other traffic. As far as he could see in either direction, no other headlights showed.

There no longer could be any doubt that this was, as he had guessed, the gold shipment. With the certainty, Wentworth's apprehensions increased. This meant, without a doubt, that he had been right in assuming that the Dragon-man would attempt a robbery of the train tonight. If the butcher could find out the date on which the treasure was to be transported, no doubt he would be able to learn, too, the precautions that would be taken and arrange to circumvent them.

If only those pilots aloft there could realize the kind of foe they faced. He had attempted to give them a clue by mentioning the slaughter at Pittsboro. They would think themselves secure against everything except attack from the air itself and believe their strength adequate to any such assault. Wentworth

Nothing but scattered wreckage was left
of the organized column of trucks!

shook his head, swore softly. What further action could he take?
Perhaps some additional warning….

IT WAS while Wentworth's hand was on the transmitter, his
eyes fixed on the tight triangle of patrolling planes, that the
thing happened. There was no warning at all, only a sudden,

blinding flash of white light, streaked with hot crimson—a gout of explosive flame against the night sky!

For a terrible instant, it hung there like some gorgeous pyrotechnic display, blinked, brightened intolerably, and was gone. Seconds afterward, the regular, triple beat of the government planes' motors still came to Wentworth, to break suddenly in a disruptive, shuddering roar that rocked the Spider's ship with the violence of the concussion… and, after that, only silence! Incredible to think that in that brief, blinding instant, three powerful ships, with their crews, had been wiped out of existence. The manner of the explosion, Wentworth did not know, but he did recognize the author. *The Dragon-man had struck again!*

Even before the concussion of the blast rocked his ship, the Spider had thrown the plane about in a tight bank and was racing toward the transport train. That destruction of the planes would signalize the attack upon the gold guards themselves. With straining eyes, Wentworth stared toward the line of headlights on the road.

For seconds, while he raced toward the trucks, nothing happened. Then, abruptly, the line was broken. A truck lurched from its place in the middle of the line, began a wild, plunging flight across the road. Its headlights blacked out. That was all, but Wentworth knew that it had plunged over the embankment and wrecked. Other trucks were running wild, the splotches of white from their headlights thrown in all directions. To Wentworth's ears came a thin stutter of gunfire.…

Wentworth spun in a *virage*, high above the road, and with a yank on the red lever, released a landing flare. An instant later, its blue-white magnesium light blazed out and revealed a scene of utmost confusion... but it was confusion without apparent cause. Five trucks were motionless on the road and three of them had been rammed from behind by others of the train. Four other trucks lay in the ditch and over these eager yellow flames were dancing.

The motorcycle and armored-car escort that had preceded the convoy raced into sight around the northward bend of the road while Wentworth turned and dived low over the road. Still there was no enemy in sight; nothing save the helpless confusion of the train, like a herd of mechanized cattle thrown into a silly stampede.

Even as Wentworth's keen eyes searched the sides of the road for the cause of this disruption, the armed escort darted near. Abruptly, the motorcycle that was in the lead swerved wildly. It crossed the road in a swift burst, struck the stone wall... Fresh gouts of flame spurted into the air and a dark hurtling form sped on to crash among close-growing trees. That was the driver.

Instantly, the same madness seemed to seize upon those other guards. Motorcycles crashed; automobiles skidded and wrecked, or stopped with such suddenness that others piled up against them. In a few seconds nothing was left of that tight, organized column speeding to the rescue of the gold trucks, except the scattered wreckage of their vehicles and a few dark huddled forms in the road.

That much Wentworth saw before the landing flare blacked out, and he saw, too, that there was no possibility of a landing place for the plane in this vertical, wooded country. His resolution was instantly formed. From its compartment in the cockpit, he detached a sub-machine gun, slung three extra drums of ammunition on straps about his neck and leveled off the plane at fifteen hundred feet. It meant the destruction of his ship, but down below, men were dying before an invisible enemy whose master could be only—the Dragon-man! The evil cohorts must be near at hand, or there would be no hope of making a getaway with the treasure. They would come by the scores and the Spider would be alone, unless Nita had succeeded... No, he could not hope for that. It was one man against the looting hordes....

Now was the time!

Wentworth's lips thinned in a bitter smile.

He cut the plane's ignition and leaped over the side, into the void where the only certainty was... death!

CHAPTER 8
THE DEATH SHOWER!

IF, IN his inner heart, Richard Wentworth hoped against hope for police to crash into his battle with the murdering hordes that awaited him, he was foredoomed. Nita van Sloan had been struggling since the moment he left her to put through her calls to the police in Pittsboro and Albany. She reached them easily enough, but she also knew they were paying no heed to her frantic warnings—knew that even before the radio brought her the fearful news of her failure, and the murderous success of the Dragon at Pittsboro and Albany.

Dull realization came to her finally that her work was not finished. Two of the Dragon's threats had been fulfilled, but there was a third. She knew, even as the thought brushed across her mind, that the man she loved was rushing into that fresh battle—into the race to prevent the Dragon from robbing the government gold train. In the face of her despairing foreknowledge of failure, Nita flung a fresh series of pleas to the police along the Hudson River; assaulting local governmental offices with her warnings. And their questions went a tedious round: Who was she? Where had she received her information? Her data would be referred to the proper authorities....

The futility of the process was maddening. If only Dick would batter some sense into these smug disbelievers! Circumstances would do that soon enough but when that happened it would be too late. She knew, with an assurance that did not have to spring from conscious thought, that Wentworth's life hung in the balance. She *must* make these fools listen....

Nita sprang to her feet and her imperative summons on the signal system brought Ram Singh, Jackson and the aged Jenkyns running to the drawing room. The butler's wrinkled face was puckered in alarm. Ram Singh's dark, loyal eyes sought out her face and clung there. But the swift, blue gaze of Jackson swept the room in one comprehensive glance, prodded at the bullet-proof French doors that gave on the terrace, before it came to rest on hers.

"I am going to Commissioner Kirkpatrick." Nita told them quietly. "Police are watching this house, as you know. We'll leave by the emergency exit. Ram Singh, you and Jenkyns will guard the house and keep communications open so that either the *sahib* or myself can reach you or relay messages through here. Jackson, you'll go with me."

Smiling eagerness was in Jackson's blue eyes. "We going to kidnap the Commissioner, Miss Nita?" he asked.

Even in her extremity, Nita could spare a smile. "If necessary," she said quietly. "I can't make the police or anyone else listen to my warnings. If we can arouse Kirkpatrick from the coma... The major—" She used the title by which Jackson preferred to call Wentworth after their war service together—"the major says that Kirkpatrick's coma is as much occult as the result of drugs. A psychic shock might revive him. We... have to try!"

She told them then of the danger that hung over Wentworth, which must come to a head long before they could reach his side, even if they knew his whereabouts. She drew in a deep breath, then lifted her head.

"If we fail with Kirkpatrick," she said firmly, "one thing remains. We will raid police headquarters and counterfeit an official order by radio and the teletype!"

THE ELEVATOR dropped Nita and Jackson to the basement and Nita focused her flashlight on a certain high corner of the furnace room, blinked it on and off in broken rhythm. Smoothly, a segment of the wall pivoted and she ran swiftly through, with Jackson just behind her. Diffused, sunken lights turned this secret passageway beneath city streets into a hospital corridor, white walls, soundless floor. Even Nita's voice was muted.

"Nothing must stop us, Jackson," she said. "There's so little time…" Her thought was with Dick then, even as his was with her in the instant that he plunged from the cockpit of his airplane, leaping into the midst of battle against unknown, but certainly desperate odds….

The tunnel came to an abrupt end against a brick wall and, in a side niche, Nita peered through a periscope into the dark tenement basement beyond. In it, nothing stirred. Nita twisted the lever that allowed the door to pivot, and Jackson slipped through ahead of her to search for hidden danger. He found none and yet Nita, standing in the darkness while the secret door swung shut, knew a moment of uncertainty, of dread….

There was no reason for it; none that she knew, so Nita insisted to herself. But it was certain enough that the Dragon, having once attempted and failed to kill them, would try again….

That thought crept on silent feet with Nita across the black basement, made her clutch the automatic she carried until her arm ached with the strain. No fresh menace developed, but it seemed to her that, as she mounted the creaking ancient stairs that led to the street floor, she was moving into the maw of danger. Yet the sounds that reached her ears, at first strange for this time and place, conveyed no hint of peril. She heard laughter, and happy shouting above the loud, pounding rhythm of a radio as if many people danced gaily in the streets.

That was Nita's first reaction. Then coldness crawled on slow, apprehensive feet along her spine and she turned to Jackson, her eyes widening in alarm. Once before tonight, she had heard such sounds of jubilation and there was an overtone here she recognized—a reckless wildness to the laughter, the shrill edge of hysteria in the shouting....

Nita drew in a slow, quivering breath. That other time, Wentworth had been beside her, and when he had challenged... he had found the trail of the Dragon! The darkness suddenly seemed alive with leering, ominous eyes. There was work here—work for the Spider's mate, to save these innocent people from the horror of the drugs that were maddening them. God, she could not! She had to save Dick! Nita thrust open the door and stepped into the sour stench of the tenement hallway....

If the slimy traces of the Dragon marked the street and its people, at least no one seemed yet smitten by the terror which tainted the very air where the Dragon moved. To outward appearance, a fiesta was in progress in this dead-end street that reached almost to the banks of the river. Gay arches of colored lights threw glamour over the dingy scene, a radio blared music and dozens of young people danced on the pavements. Children shrieked and ran about among the crowds despite the lateness of the hour while their mothers gossiped happily in groups against the tenement fronts. There were crowds, too, about the booths that dispensed food and drinks, but no one seemed to pay any attention to the men who operated them, though those men were strangers.

Perhaps that was because the men seemed kindly, though they were far from that in appearance. The booth nearest the river was operated by a weazened, small man whose expensive tailored suit was better fitted to Broadway than to this neighborhood and whose eyes held a beady, ugly glisten like a snake's.

He was certainly a man to watch closely, indeed apprehensively. And yet he seemed to love children. He was giving away free drinks to Tony Bertoldi and his companion. They seized the bottles and promptly ran off into the darkness.

"Geez, ain't this a pipe, Butch!" Tony chortled to the other boy. "I had four bottles already and ain't paid a cent yet!"

"Me, neither," Butch grinned back. "And don't these here drinks make you feel swell inside!"

"You, Tony!"

Tony whipped about, his shoulders braced against the tenement wall, while his quick eyes quested about and spotted the woman who had called him. There was something suddenly animal-like and furtive in Tony's posture. The rage that warped his face was strangely... exaggerated!

"Tony!" his mother insisted. "Where from came the money for that drink, ha? You got money to spend on drinks, you give it to me! Understand me, Tony?"

Tony fairly danced in anger. He shook both fists violently in the air. "Go to hell!" he shouted. "Go to hell, damn you!"

Tony's pleasant-faced mother stared incredulously after him as he darted into a tenement doorway and vanished with his companion. She turned hesitantly toward the woman beside her.

"It wasn't my Tony," she said slowly. "It couldn't be my Tony. He doesn't talk to me like that."

She seemed hurt, a little frightened, but she saw no reason to watch that snake-eyed man who was passing out more free drinks to other boys like Tony. Why should she?

IN THE darkly cluttered court behind the tenement, Tony

crouched behind some broken packing cases with Butch. He was staring sullenly at the ground while he polished off the drink. He was shaken by what he had done and yet that facile rage still convulsed him. Butch gurgled down the last of the drink....

"Geez!" he whispered. "Don't this stuff make you feel swell? Make you spit in your ma's eyes!" he chuckled hoarsely.

Tony was abruptly on his feet, shouting down at the startled Butch. "I don't spit in my mother's eye," he yelled thickly. "For two cents, I'd spit in your eye!"

Butch scrambled erect, too, his face crinkled in the same inordinate rage that shook Tony, the bottle clutched like a club. "You will like hell!" he snarled.

Tony struck without a word, with the viciousness of a killer, and Butch was hurled, bleeding, to the ground. Tony stood over him and struck again and again. He kicked his friend's face in. Long after life had been beaten from the boy, Tony continued to hammer at the corpse. He stopped as suddenly as he had struck, dashed the moisture from his rage-bitten lips and ran off... to the stand of the snake-eyed man.

"Give me another drink," Tony demanded violently. The tears were streaming down his face. "Another drink. This is the dope!"

The dispenser of free drinks smiled thinly in sardonic amusement. "You're right, kid," he whispered. "You're dead right!"

If Angela heard the man as she came for her drink, the words didn't mean anything to her. Her darkly vivid face was laughing up at Giuseppe.

"I been working hard as anything in pop's store all day," she confided, "but I don't feel a bit tired!" She finished off her drink

104

and Giuseppe laughed as he took her in his arms and they whirled off, dancing. "I could just dance all night," she smiled. "I don't know when I've felt so... so...."

"Hot! Just hot, baby!" Guiseppe laid his lips close against her ear. "You're just burning up, Angela!"

Angela's laughter was high, a little uncertain. "You mustn't say such things, Giu'," she whispered. "What would Father Joseph say!"

For the moment the words sobered her, but when Giuseppe led her off along another of those dark tenement hallways to the court beyond, she only laughed softly. If she had listened carefully, she might have heard other laughter that was neither Giuseppe's eager breathlessness, nor the sardonic thin mirth of Snake Eyes. It was hissing and shrill and Nita would have recognized it and understood... the laughter of the Dragon!

Angela and Giuseppe were kissing when her brother found them. His fist clamped on Giuseppe's shoulder and whirled him about. For an instant, the two men locked in battle, then Angela pushed them apart—and saw the gun glinting in Giuseppe's hand!

"No!" she cried. "No, don't kill him..." She broke into a wild, high laughter. "Why waste bullets? Listen. With your gun, we can rob a bank! We'll be rich!"

Angela's young and lovely face was hotly flushed, and her soft lips that were now parted in a wanton eagerness. "We can rob a bank," she whispered. "Think what we can buy with the money!"

The two men were frowning on her flushed loveliness, her

brother and the man who loved her. In a moment, they caught fire from the transformed girl.

"Not a bank," Giuseppe whispered presently. "Not a bank, but we could rob the market!"

Angela could not seem to stop her laughter. It rang out clear and throat-warm in the night. "We'll need more men," she cried. "Leave that to me." She flung both arms around Giuseppe's neck and glued her lips, her whole young body to his, then ran off into the darkness.

"And bring back some more drinks!" Giuseppe called after her....

Angela's laughter floated back for answer. She ran through the drab tenement hallway and, in the darkness, bumped into someone. Her hands closed on finely textured tweed cloth and for an instant she clung close, thinking, *"A man."* But it was a woman's voice that spoke to her—a low, cultured voice.

"Bank robbing is dangerous business, my dear," she said. "Far too dangerous for a fine girl like you."

Angela winced back from that voice in alarm. "Who... Who are you?" she gasped.

"Don't you know," the voice, soft as the whisper of conscience, continued, "that you aren't yourself? Angela wouldn't ever think of a thing like that. You have been drugged—doped by those free drinks!"

A muffled, shivering scream rose from Angela's lips. "Oh, who are you?" she whimpered. "How could you know such things?"

Laughter answered her, and though it was a woman that laughed, it was strangely sinister, such laughter as often had terrified the denizens of the underworld—flat, mocking, horribly full of menace—the laughter of the Spider on Nita's woman's lips!

"The Spider!" she whispered. "The Spider speaks!"

Angela fled shrieking and where she sped terror ran with her. Her voice rose high and higher, "The Spider! The Spider will kill us all!"

IN THE darkness, Nita turned to Jackson with bitterness on her mouth. "To frighten her was the only way," she said heavily. "Always duty stops us when we rush to the major's aid. We must destroy these vile concoctions of drugs before we go on. Quickly! Come with me!"

"There is no time, Miss Nita!" Jackson cried. "When we have sent help to the major, we can return to this job!"

Nita sighed, for everything in her prompted that she should follow Jackson's plea. Rebelliously, she shook her head. Surely, Dick came first! These people could wait... But even as the thought formed in her brain, Nita discarded it.

"Is that," she asked softly, "what Richard Wentworth would do if the situation were reversed? When we have done what we can to save him, it may be too late to help these people!" Nita's voice caught on a sob even as she exhorted Jackson, for she knew past any doubt that when she finished here, it would be too late to help anyone else. Well she knew that she and Jackson were about to go into battle against the forces of the Dragon!

Jackson's deep contrite voice was in her ear. "Forgive me, Miss Nita, I did not think... For the major, then!"

He thrust past Nita then and ran swiftly toward the street.

But Nita raced after him, her heels clicking like soft gunshots in the narrow hall.

"Wait!" she cried. "Wait, Jackson! We must take as few chances as possible so that when we are finished...."

Jackson checked, his breath coming noisily. "I follow where you lead, Commander," he said humbly.

The voice that thundered at them seemed to strike with a force almost physical: "Kill them! Kill every damned one of the lice!" it cried.

The gun in Nita's hand swiveled toward the sound of that voice and her finger was tight on the trigger... But she held her fire, peering out into the street from which the voice had come. Mounted on a low box, a man was gesticulating wildly while he roared out his challenge.

"We'll kill every cop we see!" he was shouting. "One of them gave me a parking-ticket today."

From the mob that had gathered before him, an angry roar went up! Nita, the gun ready in her hand, stared in bewilderment at the fury on their faces. Surely they couldn't seriously be angered to the point of murder over such a trivial thing as a ticket for parking? It seemed incredible and yet Nita knew without question that murder was their deliberate purpose... Of course! It was the drugs!

Even as the explanation came to her, there was a surging movement of the mob and some of the leaders began to race down the street bent on murdering the police! Nita sprang instantly into the street and her gun sent its imperious summons ahead of her. Its bellow stopped men dead in their tracks. White, convulsed faces turned toward her....

"Back!" Nita ordered them clearly. "Back to your holes, cowards! Does it take a mob to kill one man? Are you willing to be killed because this fool got a parking-ticket?"

Her reasonable words did not touch the men before her, or if they did only goaded them to fresh rage. With a shrill cry, the leader hurled himself straight at Nita!

JACKSON THRUST forward, his broad shoulders set in anger and a full flush rising in his strongly muscled jaws. He ducked the man's attack deftly with a straight-arm jab, sent him kicking into the gutter. It gained an instant pause and in that moment Nita caught Jackson's arm and ran before the mob— not blindly and not toward safety. She ran straight toward the booths.

"Pretend to hide in the booths," she gasped to Jackson as they fled. "The mob will wreck them looking for us, and..." She broke off as the snake-eyed man from the end booth sprang into the open with a gun in his fist.

As he leveled it, he whistled shrilly and from the swift action of the other vendors, the sound was plainly a signal. Instantly, guns flashed into sight on every side. Jackson's revolver already was thundering and Nita's added its spiteful voice. Snake-Eyes, struck in two places at the same moment, was dead before he hit the ground.

Jackson thrust Nita into the protection of a drink-stand, kept up a rapid fire against the enemy.

"Run for it," he urged her softly. "I'll hold them off while you get help for the major!"

Nita smiled her acknowledgment of his gallantry, but it was futile. The killers were on every side. Many of them had gone down under their rapid fire, but Nita knew it couldn't continue. Their enemies were too many and, crazed by drugs, were absolutely without fear. Desperately, Nita's thoughts flew to Wentworth. If only she could escape here....

"Dick," she whispered. "Oh, Dick, please..." It was like a prayer—and it brought its own curious answer. For somewhere in the night sky, there issued a fearful voice, a hissing, roaring, scream of laughter—the laughter of the Dragon!

"Down!" screamed the voice. "Down upon your faces, fools, and worship!"

Immediate silence fell on the street.

The gunmen who had been masquerading in the booths flung themselves face down and began to bump their foreheads on the ground in an abject kowtow. For the moment that was all, but every eye was turned toward the sky from whence that awful voice came.

"My slaves," the voice thundered on, "I am the bringer of your dreams. You feel brave and happy tonight because of having drunk the liquor of dreams which I have given you...."

Nita was urging Jackson to his feet while terror sent tremors over her entire body. "Move slowly," she urged softly. "Move slowly and no one will pay any attention to us..." Her voice was blotted out by the thunder from above and from the black night sky there began to filter soft bits of scarlet that fluttered as daintily as down—the petals of the Blood Orchid!

"Down, slaves!" thundered the Dragon. "Worship me... or *you die!*"

Even as that venomous scream beat down upon the people, a pleasant-faced woman beside the path Nita had chosen uttered a shriek and clutched her breast. Nothing showed there—nothing save the crimson beauty of one of the hellish flower petals! Agony warped her face. She tore at her throat with wild hands, plucked at the air and pitched writhing to the ground in the throes of death.

Before her first scream had soared to its awful climax, Nita saw a man leap into the air with the sharp blow of some unbearable pain—and he was within a yard of where she stood! There could be no doubt about it. The enemy had spotted her and Jackson and was raining death weapons down on them from above! These two people had died from wounds intended for her own and Jackson's bodies. Oh, God, she was doomed and when she fell here, Dick was doomed also....

FROM OVERHEAD, something that glittered in the brightly colored lights flashed toward her! With the quickness of despair, Nita tripped Jackson and hurled herself face-down on the ground. She heard a man cry out hoarsely as the missile missed her and struck. But she could not delay. She had seen the source of that last attempted assassination—and, like the Spider's mate, she was going to attack!

"Keep face down," she told Jackson, "and they won't be able

to recognize us! Then crawl after me! We're going to put a stop to this butchery!"

The Dragon Voice was shrieking out the same order over and over again to the slaves, and screams rent the air. On every side people pitched writhing to the ground. Nita's soft lips were pressed rigidly together as she dragged herself across the pavement. Gone was her fear and there remained only the grim determination to stop these killers and to take vengeance for those who had died.

Dick... Dick's strength fought with her, she knew. This was the course he himself would have taken, she was sure, and the thought buoyed her up. She was almost in the shadow of the tenement now and though her hands and knees were torn from crawling, a fierce happiness welled up in her. With a brief, eager cry, that was like the fighting yell of the Spider himself, she sprang to her feet and charged into the dark hallway of the tenement.

Nita caught the stair railing and threw herself upward, gun ready in her fist and the swift beat of Jackson's supporting race just behind her. On the roof, she would tangle with Dick's foes, perhaps even the Dragon himself! If she could find and kill *him*... Her breath came sobbingly as she forced herself up the creaking flights of stairs. The screams of the dying rang in her ears.

"Let me go first!" Jackson pleaded, running behind her. "If anything happened to you...."

Nita laughed with gasping breath. If anything happened to her... and in the street, scores had been stricken. He could think of that now! She reached the top floor and flung herself at the ladder that spanned the last gap to the roof. Hard hands gripped her shoulders and hurled her aside and, at the same instant, a gun threw its crimson spear of deadly flame down from the roof!

The probing finger of fire from Jackson's revolver answered, and up there in the darkness a man shrieked his death-cry. Nita felt a tremor of dread strike her but she did not pause. While that scream stabbed into her brain, she was back at the ladder. This time Jackson had gone on ahead. His gun was already speaking.

Nita thrust her head above the level of the roof and immediately was shooting at top speed. Dark huddled figures returned her bullets and she heard the savage crunch of lead biting into the wooden frame that half-concealed her!

It was a blurred hell of murder for Nita but presently the guns were still and she could clamber weakly to her feet beside Jackson. Already he was running toward the low wall that fronted on the street. Nita staggered after him while she fumblingly reloaded her automatic. There were the bodies of men she had helped to kill scattered about her, but she gazed on them without compunction. These were the men who had slain those helpless people in the street, who had tried to kill her and Jackson....

Jackson whirled from the roof-edge and at once Nita caught tension in the taut lines of his brawny body. "The police," his sharp-pitched low voice reached her. "Squads of police. They're already filling the street below!"

FOR A moment, Nita stared without comprehension at him. They had no reason to fear the police, surely... Then a slow and bitter smile touched her lips. They had been here where men had been killed, hadn't they? They were here now in the spot from whence had come the death that struck down the people below. Even if they escaped blame for the deaths, they would be delayed for hours and that could not be. It might already be too late to save Dick....

Stumbling with her sudden fatigue, Nita turned toward the coping by which they had reached the roof. "Back the way we came," she said dully. "Our only chance now is to retreat to the mansion and escape from it by another way. God! I hope we're in time!"

Nita was aware of Jackson's supporting arm about her as they reeled down the ladder and made their hurried way down steps that seemed to shriek aloud a warning to the police that here fled the Spider's mate! She heard men's shouts in the street, caught a glimpse of a squad of blue-coated men charging toward her. Then the grateful blackness of the basement swallowed her and she was blinking her flashlight on the hidden door that would lead her back to the safety of Dick's house. Jackson helped her through the door and it clapped shut just as light blazed out in the cellar behind... but it was in ample time. Nita leaned her back against the door, panting. She was safe. Yes, but defeated also, driven back from the course she had set herself to save Dick. She must hurry....

Along the muted corridor, Nita ran and the silenced beat of her feet seemed to thud inside her own brain, hammering out words she knew and feared, "Defeat... defeat... hurry... hurry..." She flung herself into the elevator and jabbed the button that would send it upward, conscious of Jackson, grave-faced, beside her.

"I've got a funny feeling," he said hoarsely. "Something has gone wrong, I'm afraid. It's just the way I feel. You let me go first. The major will hold me responsible if anything happens...."

He threw open the elevator doors and a great cry tore itself out of his throat. Nita put out a groping hand and kept herself from falling while her eyes stared wider and wider at what lay on the floor at their feet.

Jackson hurled himself down on his knees there, but Nita reeled past him and peered down the length of the drawing-room. Then and then only did Nita admit that not only defeat but disaster had entered the house of Richard Wentworth. For prostrate in the hall lay the body of faithful old Jenkyns and against the terrace door which he had guarded to the last lay Ram Singh. From the breast of each sprouted the Blood Orchid!

Tears welled to Nita's eyes, tears for these brave men who had died because of their loyalty, but strangely the sound that came from her throat was not a sob. It was a cough! It shook Nita, bowed her double with its violence, but to Nita it meant nothing in particular. To Wentworth it would have told another more fearful story. He had heard that cough before this on the lips of doomed men, and those who coughed had shortly died... with the Blood Orchid on their breasts!

CHAPTER 9
GOLDEN DEATH

WHEN WENTWORTH, leaping blindly in his parachute, to the rescue of the men who were transporting the government gold, was flung finally to earth, he found himself several hundred yards to the south of the wreckage of the trucks and above the road upon the brow of almost perpendicular hills. There was a worried frown between his eyes, for what he had seen below him—trucks and men running wild without apparent cause—was a puzzle. He knew only that some new and fearful weapon had been loosed by the Dragon upon these men, for the spores of the Blood Orchid did not work so swiftly....

On the chance that this weapon might be gas, Wentworth donned the atmosphere mask he carried always in his plane, though he thought that he was above the reach of such vapors here upon the brink of the hill. He cradled his machine-gun in his arms, ready for immediate use, and ran through the cold and brittle woods toward the scenes of destruction he had glimpsed from above. Ahead of him, he caught a high wailing cry, a signal of some sort. He cut his speed, moved almost silently along the crest of a low ridge that had been sliced in half for the passage of the highway. He crept to the verge of the cut, peered down... and swore viciously under his breath.

From deep ravines on the sides of the road, men were stealing swiftly toward the trucks and in their hands he caught the gleam of sharp steel. Even as Wentworth watched, one of them stooped over the huddled form of one of the gold guards and the steel flashed home! Wentworth jerked up the submachine gun, yet hesitated.

There was something curious about these sneaking forms of men. Their hands seemed enormous and there was no shape to their heads which seemed straight-sided, rising enormous as helmets or heavy hoods and extending almost to the line of their shoulders.

It might be some species of armor against which his bullets would be useless... Still, he could not stand idly by, with a weapon in his hand, while they slaughtered any of the guards who might remain alive!

Once more, Wentworth lifted the machine gun in readiness... and heard a twig crack behind him! Wentworth hurled himself violently to one side, rolled. He was in the nick of time. Almost on the spot where he had crouched stood one of the curiously garbed looters and a foot-long knife glittered in his hand as it swept down! Wentworth had not fallen without a plan in mind and, the instant his rolling shoulders hit earth, he struck out with both feet. There was no miscalculation. His feet buried themselves in the stomach of the assassin, drove him writhing to the ground. In a trice, Wentworth was upon him, wresting the knife free.

With a wrench, he tore at the helmet, which proved strangely soft and yielding to his hand. He drove a hard fist to the jaw of the captured Chinese, before he paused to investigate. Then, he found to his surprise, he held only a broad-brimmed hard-straw hat from which a close-meshed net had been draped—such an outfit as bee-keepers wear to prevent stings! Wentworth stared blankly at the net, then lifted a hand to rub clean the lens of his gas mask and make sure there was no mistake. A bee net... But surely, the gold train had not been wrecked by a mere release of bees!

GRIMLY, WENTWORTH bound his prisoner and afterward, with quick movements, donned the bee net and heavy gloves which the assassin had worn. They would make an excellent disguise, perhaps even permit him to move among the killers themselves without detection! Wentworth caught up the long-bladed knife, clutched the machine-gun under his short coat and slipped down the steep side of the cut.

Apparently, the work of slaughter had been finished. The motors were roaring again in those trucks which had not been wrecked and, as Wentworth reached the roadside, they began a laborious turn to travel back the way they had come. Other men were moving over the wreckage of the cars that had gone into the ditch, and were swiftly emptying them of their heavy cargo. But they made no effort to load it into the other trucks. Instead, two men would sling a gold-loaded box upon a pole, rest it on their shoulders and trot swiftly into the woods toward the river!

For a moment, Wentworth hesitated in the shadows. A few bursts of machine-gun fire would send the Chinese fleeing to cover. He might even be able to stand off attack until state police or other officials hurried here, summoned by the sound of gunfire, or perhaps by the explosion of those overhead planes, in which the Dragon undoubtedly had planted bombs. Wentworth knew enough about the organization of such convoys

to realize that there must have been arrangements for radio reports at least every fifteen minutes. How many had passed since that fatal blast in mid-air? Wentworth shook his head. Impossible to estimate exactly. Certainly, no more than fifteen....

Behind the bee-net, Wentworth's eyes took on a steely light. His course was plain. Within a few minutes at most, these men would have completed their looting of the trucks, unless he stopped them. They would flee then with the gold, back to the master of all this evil, back to the Dragon himself! To find and slay that monster was vastly more important than saving this shipment of gold, however valuable it might be. In the bee-net disguise, it might be possible for the Spider to masquerade as one of the Chinese. Of course, there was the ever-present danger that one of the men would recognize and slip twelve inches of steel in between his shoulders....

With swift hands, Wentworth deposited all save one of the machine-gun drums under a bush and contrived to sling the weapon itself, with its one drum detached and flat against his side, beneath his loose-hanging coat. That done, the steel still in his fist, Wentworth trotted out to join the Chinese.

He did not depend exclusively on the veil for disguise. His head was bowed, his shoulders stooped and his short-stepping stride, all were typical of the coolies he sought to imitate. WENTWORTH HURRIED toward a truck that was overturned in a ditch, whose askew lights still threw their beams across the blackness of the night. In that light, Wentworth caught sight of small, flying darts of black and, as he trotted forward, one of them struck against his face-net, clung there, buzzing angrily. It was a bee, even as he had half-guessed, but it showed such fury as no insect Wentworth had ever seen before. It fought to get through the net and reach him while it struck again and again at the cloth with its sting!

Wentworth brushed the thing aside with his thickly gloved hand, trotted on.

The body of one of the guards lay sprawled, half in the head-light glare, and Wentworth saw to his amazement that the man's body literally crawled alive with bees! Where his flesh was visible, it showed discolored, horribly swollen... and suddenly Wentworth knew the truth. The stings of these bees had been poisoned!

For some reason, whose secret the Dragon undoubtedly held, these bees would attack human beings, viciously. With what horrible subtlety the Dragon worked! Plainly, he had released swarms of these fierce bees, with their poison stings, to fly across the road. Even when they got into the cabs of the trucks, the guards would not have suspected an attack. It would be merely an annoyance, something to curse over even if they were stung—until the deadly and sudden poison was burning in their veins. And then it would be too late!

The air was full of the deadly little pests, but the Chinese seemed to pay them no heed. In fact, Wentworth could not see that any of them were molested by the bees though occasionally one of the men would brush a hand across the net that hung before his face… Wentworth trotted into a chain of the Chinese at the tail of the wrecked truck and, at a grunted order, took one end of a pole to which a box of gold had been slung.

It was an art in itself, a part of every coolie-porter's training, to be able to run in pairs with a heavy load on a pole between them—without throwing undue weight upon their fellow, or with little jarring. It was a matter of rhythm in the stride, in the swing of the load they carried, and Wentworth saw his problem instantly. Yet it was one he must meet successfully if he were to fulfill his plan of tracking the gold to its end in the vaults of the Dragon—and eliminating the Dragon for all time!

He had managed to take the rear position under the pole and, with the perfect coordination of his trained muscles, managed to imitate so far as he could see the trot of the coolie ahead of him. The man cried out at him angrily in a dialect Wentworth did not understand, and Wentworth snarled back at him, unintelligibly. Out of his eye corners, he glanced at other pairs carrying their loads, but he could not detect whatever secret trick enabled them to move in perfect rhythm.

At the same time, Wentworth became conscious of another thing. Though the bees left the Chinese comparatively unbothered, more and more of them were gathering around him! The mesh of his net was becoming encrusted with them. When he brushed some aside, others took their places immediately, and the air was filled with the thick angry buzz of their wings!

Wentworth caught at the answer to this mystery, even as he spotted ahead a Chinese foreman standing at the brink of the hill that sloped to the river. For some reason… to which the

Dragon would hold the answer—the bees left Chinese alone, but were infuriated in the presence of a white man! If the foreman ahead knew this fact, the Spider's masquerade was already destroyed!

Desperately, as he neared the man at the brink of the hill, Wentworth swept the bees aside and strove to attain the porter's rhythm. His eyes stabbed at the face behind the net but he could see only shadows there. If the foreman were suspicious, Wentworth would know it only when he had passed—and the foreman's ready knife had struck! Yet, to make good his subterfuge and reach the Dragon lair, he must take his chances.

Nearing the brink of the hill. Wentworth could peer down into the river and see a half-dozen low-lying speed boats lined up there. The motors were idling gently and, as he watched, one of them swung out into the current in a wide circle and raced off downriver toward New York City. Abruptly, from the woods, a brilliant shaft of light licked out and bathed Wentworth in its full glare! He heard a voice crack out fiercely, shouting....

"A foreign devil! A spy! Kill! *Kill! Kill!*"

AT THE first stab of that light, Wentworth sprang into action. He dropped his load, hurled the knife he carried straight at the nearby foreman and, before the blade could strike, Wentworth doubled on his tracks and streaked back across the road toward the place where he had hidden his extra submachine gun ammunition. The coolies about the trucks suddenly formed in an attacking gang and charged toward him with uplifted knives, cutting off his retreat. Knives began to flicker through the air, hurled with deadly accuracy.

Wentworth hit the concrete pavement in a dive, rolled and brought up hard against the stone wall at its side. He was over it in a single fluid movement and his hands flew beneath his coat, whipped out the sub-machine gun. It was awkward, working with the thick gloves, but he dared not remove them. The bees of the poison stings buzzed about his head.

True, he had automatics beneath his arms but that armament would be too weak to beat back this wholesale attack. There were twenty, thirty men in plain sight and perhaps as many more lurking in the woods! He had the gun and drum of cartridges free now of the fastenings by which he had slung them beneath his coat. He was trying to snap the ammunition-clip into place.

Just beyond the wall, a multiple shout went up. Feet brushed the top of the wall and, just over Wentworth, a powerful figure of a Chinese towered. With a shrill cry, knife-first, the man dived at him. Wentworth's feet were doubled under him and his leap aside came with a mere, swift straightening of his legs. The knife ripped across his sleeve... and a touch of cold dread touched Wentworth's heart. If the bees should find that opening, even all his bullets would not keep death at bay!

Clutching the still useless gun to his chest, Wentworth darted into the cover of the trees. The brilliant searchlight swung toward him, sent shafted shadows swirling across his path, alternating with beams of dazzling white. He crouched at the base of a tree, rapidly knotted a handkerchief over the tear in his sleeve. The Chinese were creeping shadows in the dark, coming at him from all sides. But now at last, he had the sub-machine gun ready.

On stealthy feet, he moved back toward the stone wall....

A knife flickered through light and shadow and buried three inches of its keen blade in a tree beside Wentworth's head. He braced himself and swung the nose of the machine-gun. Screams broke out in the underbrush. Men groveled in dying convulsions and a few fled, but there were plenty of others—and half his drum of ammunition was gone! On frantic feet, Wentworth raced for the stone wall. A man loomed in his path and Wentworth squeezed on the trigger. The stab of flame from the gun's muzzle seemed to hammer the man aside like a rod of steel. Ah, the wall was just ahead!

Wentworth went over it in a high hurdle and, instantly, bullets were skimming the concrete from a firing party crouched behind the ruins of one of the trucks. Lead hissed past his ears, hit the pavement and ricocheted with a high, angry whine. One of those mutilated bullets could tear off half a man's face! Wentworth's sub-machine gun centered, and he rode the trigger, throwing his weight against the rising recoil of the weapon. He saw a Chinese tower to his feet atop the wrecked truck, hands clawing at the sky, silhouetted against the strong, reaching beam of the searchlight. He saw another pitch headlong to the road. He waited for no more.

With long bounds, he crossed the concrete road and dived into the underbrush. His drum was almost empty now. If there was another mass attack, he was finished. There was flashing fire in the Spider's eyes now. His plan for merging with the Dragon's force was defeated in its inception; he would show them how the Spider could fight! The flight with the gold was stopped. All the trucks that could be moved had already gone, but there were still four trucks in the ditch and those boats upon the river. That much he could save—and would.

In the darkness, Wentworth found his reserve drums of ammunition and his lips twisted in a thin smile. He sent his mocking, flat laughter into the darkness.

"Come on, you hatchet men!" he taunted them in the Mandarin dialect. "Come on, you killers of foreign devils! The Spider awaits you—and his stings, too, are poisoned!"

He loosed a burst of machine-gun bullets along the crest of the stone wall across the roadway, sent another scouring the ditch and the wrecks of the trucks. A small group of Chinese sprang to their feet and raced for the cover of the woods beyond. They did not reach it. Wentworth was on his feet now, crouched over the spitting gun, ammunition drums swinging from his shoulders. Here was some small vengeance for the slaughter that had been enacted this night! If he could not reach the Dragon himself, at least he could decimate his forces—retrieve a portion of the loot.

Bounding, Wentworth reached the crest of the hill path that led down to the boats, no more than a hundred and fifty yards away. His gun would not be highly accurate at that range, but it had no need to be. The spray of bullets would serve instead. He whipped the water to a froth with lead, heard men scream and saw some plunge into the river to escape.

A punctured gasoline tank spewed liquid flame over two of the boats. A third speedster spurted for the middle of the river but the howling bullets of the Spider went faster yet. The man who crouched over the wheel sprang straight up, screaming, and fell across the thwarts. The boat cut a fast, sharp circle in mid-stream, surged back against the boats that remained. With a splintering crash, it rammed home.

There were no more boats now; only a few dark, swimming heads in the river to mark the raiding scores that the Dragon had sent to collect government gold. Wentworth snapped on a fresh drum of ammunition and once more scoured the woods with bullets. There was no answering scream or shot... Stiffly, Wentworth drew himself erect. His breath was coming noisily through distended nostrils, and there was a blaze in his eyes.

Yes, it was vengeance, punishment of a kind, but no adequate answer to such a butcher as the Dragon. By God, that monster should know that the penalties of his crimes would seek him out at the ruthlessly just hands of the Spider!

Wentworth reached the side of one of the dead Chinese in two strides and bent to grind into the dead flesh of his forehead the seal of the Spider. Let the Dragon know who had struck at him, and realize what was to come!

THE SUB-MACHINE gun slung across his shoulders, Wentworth salvaged one of the escort motorcycles and kicked its motor to life; bent far forward over the handlebars as he sent it racing down the hill. At the first possible moment, he would sound the alarm which would send police to the scene of the mass murder and the robbery of the gold trucks. But more important than that was the pursuit of the killers themselves. He had seen their trucks head this way... Ten miles down the river, Wentworth came to the end of this fresh trail of the Dragon. The trucks stood abandoned by a dock, and Wentworth was left with only the knowledge that this gold also had been trans-shipped by water.

He reached a phone in Peekskill and warned the police of New York City to be on the lookout—and barely got out of the town before he heard the siren whine of other police, summoned by radio, attempting to trap him. He recalled by a violent effort that it had been no more than twelve hours since he had received that odd warning from Fu-Chang, the scarlet scorpion—less than that since Jackson had warned him that his name and description had been broadcast to New York City's police for immediate arrest!

Wentworth wheeled his motorcycle into narrow back roads and bored on toward New York. Jackson and Nita might have some fresh clue on which he could work; some lead that would point the way to the hideout of the Dragon himself. He must join forces with them at the first possible moment, press on the attack, vigorously. By swift and furious assaults, he might be able to prevent farther depredations by the Dragon until such time as he could be tracked down!

Wentworth was low over the handlebars, pushing the motorcycle to the last atom of speed and he saw, vaguely, that his headlights seemed dim. That was the first notice he had that dawn was gray in the East.

He felt weariness in his joints, in the stiff slowness of his thoughts. Somewhere behind, after he had left the area where the poisoned bees flew, but before he had phoned to the police his warning about the bees and the raid on the gold, he had thrown aside the bee-net and hat.

He had administered a heavy defeat to the Dragon, perhaps shaken the morale of his fighting forces. There was no doubt that the Dragon would retaliate, and Wentworth, as the defender, could pick the scene of that assault! He could lay traps for the Dragon and his men... For the first time in hours, a slight, tired smile touched Wentworth's lips. All hope was not lost. If only the police could be staved off. Wentworth could lie in wait for the Dragon in the Spider's own fortified mansion. There he could defy enemies many times more potent than this Chinese trickster! Yes, there was hope. Victory might lie just around the corner....

Wentworth abandoned the motorcycle at the first opportunity and went, by means of the unsuspected subway, toward his own home. In the red light of the rising sun, he made his way into a tenement two full blocks from his home and, in its basement, opened a secret door in the brick wall. This was one thing he had copied long ago from his Chinese enemies, and friends—the secret underground entrance to his place of refuge!

The passage dipped sharply beneath the street, began to ascend. Eventually, he reached a spot where he could peer into the lighted basement of his own residence. It was empty and he sprang out of the tunnel with a sense of jubilation. He would have allies now again, and for once the Spider felt the need of assistants.

Yet, even in his elation, he moved cautiously. It was possible the police had forced an entrance here, though there was no reason why Nita should not have allowed them to search and depart. He slipped into a small, hidden closet to listen. Soundtaps led here from all over the house and would bring him the movements of everyone within it. Wentworth clamped on the ear-phones and began to move cams that would connect the rooms one by one with his listening post.

Abruptly, he coughed, and shook his head irritably. He was overtired, of course, but that was no new thing. It had been years since a cold had bothered him. Surely, he wasn't catching one? He shook his head and an eager smile was on his lips. He should hear some evidence of Nita's presence soon, She would be singing... No, not that, since she knew he was perhaps in danger. Nor would she be asleep. Waiting, of course, with Jackson and Ram Singh taking turns at guard. Jenkyns might be in the kitchen....

Wentworth coughed again, but this time he did not notice it. He had thrown the cams of half the rooms in the house without discovering any evidence of occupancy! A worried frown touched his forehead and the faintest suspicion of dread touched cold to his heart.

"Nonsense," he muttered roughly to himself. "Nothing is wrong."

THE ECHO of those words beat in his heart as he rapidly threw the rest of the cams of the system; then went swiftly over them again, room by room. Anxiously, he tested the mechanism, but it was all properly connected. Yet... not a sound in the house! Terror had its rough way with him then. With a half-muffled shout, he flung from the listening-post and began to race up the steps into his home. Before he had taken a half-dozen steps, his calm mind was at work again, soothing his fears. This was nonsense. The house might perhaps be empty, but the worst that could happen would be that police had arrested Nita and the rest on some trumped-up charge.

The echo of his own thought reached Wentworth's full consciousness. *The worst that can happen!* In heaven's name, what did he fear had happened? But he knew—yes, he *knew!* He feared that the Dragon....

Wentworth did not complete the thought. Instead, he raced wildly from room to room. He began to call Nita's name as he ran. He reached the third floor and he pounded his shouting way along the hall, into the living-room and... stopped. He stopped like a frozen statue with a distorted face—with a madman's face.

Nita was in the drawing-room. She lay upon the davenport across the room from him, but her eyes did not turn to salute him, and there was no animation in her body. None.

"Nita!"

Wentworth heard his own voice, broken and frantic, as he shouted her name, and there was no answer. He walked across the room like an automaton, with stumbling, uncertain stride until he stood over Nita where she lay motionless upon the davenport. That was when he broke. That was when the cold and implacable being, whom the world knew as the Spider, went to pieces. His face puckered like a puzzled, suffering child's and his knees went lax beneath him. He slumped down on the floor and still his eyes could not break the fascinated stare that tied them to Nita—to the thing on Nita's breast, to the scarlet and awful bloom of the Blood Orchid there....

AND IT was on Wentworth's ears that words presently began to beat—words that came from a small green Buddha enthroned upon a scarlet orchid, a statuette that had never been in his home before but which now stood in a place of honor in a table shrine.

"So you know, Richard Wentworth," came the hissing mockery of the Dragon Voice from the Buddha. "So you know now that it does not pay to fight the Dragon! All your abominable country shall know it soon! I have finished my work for the present and shall leave the vile shores of this land, leave with all my slaves and the wealth you have so kindly provided... But I only leave to prepare for my return as conqueror! And your country shall welcome me, Spider! Welcome the 'Giver of Dreams!' I shall leave men behind who will continue that efficient work while I am gone. But you don't speak, Spider. Surely, you hear me?"

Wentworth sat beside Nita, as motionless as a statue of stone. If he heard, he gave no sign. The Dragon Voice laughed softly, jarringly.

"What—dead already, Wentworth?" it asked. "I thought you were made of sterner stuff. But then I do not mind. Broken, you will make a better slave, for soon you shall be my slave, Wentworth. Did you know that yet? Haven't you been *coughing*, Richard Wentworth—since you entered your home? Just a little as yet, of course, but it will grow worse and, before the hour is out... Listen carefully, Wentworth! *Before the hour is out, you, too, shall have the red flower of the orchid on your breast!*"

For an instant, something like rationality stirred in Wentworth's face. He coughed hollowly and, subconsciously, pressed the palm of his hand to his chest, but his eyes never left one thing—and that one thing alone crowded his brain: Nita with that hellish bloom growing from her soft white breast! As if he could see the hopeless, beaten man beside his dead, the Dragon broke into his mocking, hissing laughter, and the horror of it filled the room....

CHAPTER 10
ONE HOUR TO LIVE!

THERE HAD been times in the past when Wentworth had thought Nita slain. He had seen his enemies prepare to torture her and always, somehow, he had found the strength to carry on. But to be hammered to his knees by the sudden, pitiful sight of her... Even the mockery of the Dragon seemed incapable of arousing the Spider. He appeared scarcely to breathe and yet life must be working in that motionless figure. Once, he coughed.

At the hollow vibration of that cough, the figure that was Richard Wentworth trembled. His face twitched and with stiff mechanistic movements he rose to his feet; his face twitched and settled into a stone-like mold, awful in its expressionless quality. From an eye corner, a tear pushed out and slid slowly down beside his nose, made its wet tracery to his mouth corner. He was not weeping. His face was too terrible, too set for that, and his eyes stared stonily before him. Those fixed eyes swung to the Buddha on the table, his lips moved....

One hour to live. Good God, there was not even time for vengeance. Not even... Once more, Wentworth's eyes swung back to the still, sweet figure on the davenport. He stooped over her and pressed the breathless lips. He patted the crisping hair.

"Don't worry, dear," Wentworth said hoarsely. "Don't worry. I...."

He left the sentence hanging in the air. He bent his head and drew out his two automatics, weighed them on his palms. His accustomed fingers fumbled over them, making sure of the loadings; then he thrust them back into their holsters. His legs swung. It was like that, as if his legs moved him without conscious volition on his part; a stone man walking. The tears still ran their slow way across his cheeks... There was so little time.

Mechanically, Wentworth chose the secret way by which he had entered to leave his home and, minutes later, was stalking through the quiet halls of Dr. Ridley's home. A servant had fallen back, frightened at his aspect, and now the nurse who sat beside the room of Commissioner Stanley Kirkpatrick started to her feet.

"Did you want Doctor Ridley?" she asked hurriedly.

When Wentworth did not answer, she took a slow step backward, then another... She turned and ran swiftly and her voice fluted ahead of her, calling Dr. Ridley. Wentworth turned into Kirkpatrick's room and stood over the bed where his friend lay, breast rising in slow and heavy labor of breathing in his unnatural sleep. Wentworth bent over and spoke hoarsely.

"Kirk," he said harshly. "Kirk, Nita is dead!"

His voice was low and yet the sound of it rasped through

THE DRAGON

FU CHANG

the room, reached out into the hall, where quick, slippered feet were hurrying.

"Kirk!" Wentworth said again. "Kirk, Nita is dead!"

The sleeping man's face twitched and a hand stirred. Dr. Ridley came striding in through the door, but the accent of those words stopped him. He turned to the nurse.

"It's all right," he said. "There's just a chance that shocking news will break the hypnosis, but… Good God, Dick! Did you mean that? Nita… Nita *dead?*"

Wentworth's face twisted in a spasm of anger. He struck Kirkpatrick heavily across the face. "Nita is dead!" he shouted. "Do you hear, Kirk? Nita is dead, and I am dying. You've got to come back! Somebody must…."

Kirkpatrick's eyes opened and stared blankly at Wentworth

THE BLOOD ORCHID

HWANG YO

as the voice ran on, breaking with its rasping harshness, dinning words at his friend. A convulsive shudder shook Kirkpatrick's body, and a light of sanity touched his eyes. He sat up laboriously.

"Dick," he said. "Dick! In God's name, what's the matter?"

Wentworth's hands, that seemed gaunt, already shrunken by death, reached out and caught his shoulders. "Nita is dead," Wentworth whispered, "and I'm dying. There's nothing anyone can do, but listen… listen carefully. What I can do to catch the Dragon and kill him, I will do. When I leave off… it will be your task. Do you hear, *you must kill the Dragon!*"

Bewilderment was on Kirkpatrick's face, but he spoke quietly, "Yes, Dick. I hear."

"Promise! You will kill the Dragon!"

"I promise," Kirkpatrick said quietly. "Now, Dick, you must rest!"

Wentworth sprang back from the bed and his guns were suddenly in his hands. "Damn you! Don't you understand? I have an hour to live! Now, listen!" Swiftly, in explosive, fierce words, he told what he knew of the Dragon and, if Wentworth had not consciously heard, then his subconscious brain had made a record of the last threats uttered by the Dragon. "I'm going now," he concluded. "If I can reach the Dragon before I fall, I will. If I fail, the job is yours!" He backed toward the door. "I'll kill the man who follows me!"

IN THE hall, he whirled and ran. He had a long trail to follow and the time was so short… so short. At the door, he sprang to the wheel of the car he had taken from one of the hidden garages he had scattered about the city, and bore the accelerator to the floor.

He heard a shout ring out behind him, but nothing could stop the Spider. For now he wore the Spider's make-up. Nothing... A cough came tearing up from his lungs. It strained his throat, sent congested blood to his face. He held grimly to the wheel while the paroxysm died, and there was a touch of fear in those glacial eyes. Not fear of death. He had faced it too often to flinch now from the grim face of the spectre. No, it was fear that death would come... too soon!

Wentworth was following a trail that an opium-drunk man had given him... God, was it only last night?... Twice, the Dragon had boasted of his enslavement of the people through opium—once to Nita, once a few short minutes before to him over his accursed Buddha wireless. That boy had had "just a little fun at the Red Dragon...."

The Red Dragon Inn was a tawdry place by daylight. Gaudy signs pointed the way to its second-story dining-room; its doors were locked. But on the door was posted a name and telephone number. *In emergency, phone Sam May, Chinatown Exchange.*

Wentworth flung back to the car and raced through the still half-deserted streets of early morning. The minutes crawled past, thudded by like the quickening beat of his heart. How long now? How long since he had first coughed? Easily a half of his last hour had sped. And how long before the death, sprouting within him, would cripple his strength so that he could no longer go on? A harsh curse squeezed out between Wentworth's lips.

Damn them—they could not stop him! Not Death itself should stop him before he had taken vengeance!

The home of Sam May was on the third floor of a Chinatown tenement and its slattern halls were dark and fetid with the close-living human beings who crowded them. Wentworth was not deceived. He knew that behind such impoverished hallways as these, the richest of Eastern luxury could burgeon. He pulled to a sudden halt before the door he sought and now there was stealth in his every movement, and even his rasping breath was silenced. From the vertical pocket of a leathern girdle about his waist, he slipped a slim, hooked tool of surgical steel and slid it into the keyhole of the door. An instant's manipulation with the lock-pick and the bolt slid back. Wentworth whipped the door open and found, as he had expected, a second portal within, richly carven from solid teak.

There was no keyhole here. The Chinese delighted in such puzzles. The opening of the door would be simple if one knew what bits of the carving to manipulate, but the Spider had no time to fathom its intricacies. His heavy guns sprang to his hands! A step backward and they began to speak. Four, five, six heavy shots pounded out in that close hallway. Somewhere, a woman screamed, its shrillness striking even through the roaring concussion of the guns.

Wentworth hurled himself violently against the teak-wood, and the bullets had done their work. The hinges ripped loose and he lunged through into a narrow hallway whose walls were hung in silks, in precious, embroideries of the East—in a thousand Oriental treasures.

His knowledge of Chinese custom stood him in good stead now. He knew in just which room to look for the master of this household. His long strides took him to the door, past its precise screen, set to bar out the evil spirits which all Chinese fear—which, as every Chinese knows, can travel only in straight lines....

A long stride took Wentworth to the bed where a pudgy Chinese was just lifting his body heavily from sleep. From his pocket, Wentworth whipped a thin, platinum cigarette lighter. He seized one of Sam May's hands and, into the soft flesh of its back, he ground the crimson seal of the Spider!

"Unless you wish that seal on your dead forehead," Wentworth said to him raspingly in Chinese, "you will talk and talk straight, Sam May!"

The Chinese lifted his heavy lidded eyes to the stony face above him—the harshly stern face with its wet tracery of tears. Sam May's teeth chattered in sudden abject terror.

"Where did you get the opium which you fed your guests last night?" Wentworth asked softly: "Where is the Dragon?"

"No savvy Dlagon!" Sam May chattered. "Opium sent to me by velly good fliend, Mu-Piang! You go ask Mu-Piang, please, Spider *san!*"

Truth was in his trembling terror and, without a word, Wentworth spun from the room, took the stairs from the tenement in leaping strides. Seconds... Seconds held the difference between success and failure. Wentworth did not even sheathe his guns as he went, long-striding, through Chinatown's twisted streets; nor did he pause to use a lock-pick on the dusty glass door of

Mu-Piang's shop. A gun smashed out the pane, raked splintered fragments from the frame and Wentworth was running again, along dim hallways, into the sleeping cubicle of Mu-Piang!

AS HE crossed the sill, he sensed more than saw movement at his left and flung himself aside while his gun swiveled, blasted into the dimness. The stab of gunfire showed him his foe, showed a half-naked Chinese pinned against the wall by his lead—face contorted even while his palsied knife arm strove to hurl the blade. In the darkness that slammed down again after that brief flame-light, Wentworth heard the heavy thud of the falling body. He threw the beam of his flash into the gloom and found the bed of Mu-Piang. In the wall behind it, a narrow, hidden door was just closing!

Wentworth's gun blasted again, throwing the quarter-ton impact of lead against the mechanism that worked the door. He was scarcely a fifth of a second later in ramming his shoulder through the opening, and he was in time. As he wriggled through, the light in his hand probed out a second time and his gun hammered, threw its deafening concussion against his ears.

"Halt!" Wentworth shouted. "Stop, or the next bullet smashes your spine!"

The fleeing figure of a Chinese halted, stood with trembling arms uplifted. Staggering, half-dazed by the closeness of that heavy blast, Wentworth reeled down the corridor and whirled the man around.

"You were packing, Mu-Piang," the Spider said harshly. "All your goods are stored and ready to leave. Did you go to join the Dragon, Mu-Piang? Speak, fool, or you shall this minute ascend the Dragon with your ancestors, miserable turtles! Speak, the Spider commands you!"

Mu-Piang sagged to his knees, "This humble one..." he quavered.

"Speak!" Wentworth whispered and a clawed hand reached toward the Chinese. "You were fleeing... where?"

"To the ship, Spider *san,*" Mu-Piang gasped. "It was my orders. To the *Queen Victoria.*"

Wentworth drew in a slow, heavy breath, fought the cough that surged upward from his tortured lungs. The Dragon had said, "I am leaving the vile shores of this country, taking with me my slaves and the wealth you have so kindly provided."

The cough shook Wentworth to his knees, but his eyes held implacably on the old Chinese before him, his gun was unwavering. Finally, he could get out words. God, time was so short! "The Dragon," he whispered. "The Dragon sails on the *Queen Victoria!*"

"Me not knowing," Mu-Piang said hoarsely and Wentworth was conscious of the fierce watchfulness of his eyes; of the laughter that lurked behind those black pupils. Mu-Piang knew what death loomed for the Spider! "Me telling truth, Spider *san.* You listen. Me not liking Dlagon...."

Wentworth ground the heel of his hand that held the light against his breast. There was pain there, incredible pain. His breath came hoarsely from his lips, but there was a terribly clarity in his brain. Mu-Piang recognized the swift approach of his death, was delaying him, but by the same token, in his assurance, he might be telling the truth as he said. It would appeal to his

Chinese sense of humor, damn him, to tell the truth with the sure knowledge that Wentworth would never live to act upon it. Deliberately, Wentworth made his seizure seem worse than it was. He leaned weakly against the wall while the coughing shook him again.

"Talk!" he whispered weakly. "Talk! I still can kill you!"

Mu-Piang's lips almost smiled. "Me talk," he said humbly. "Today, tonight maybe, Dlagon capture all steamers in harbor. His men sail them away. Much gold on ships. Need many ships to carry his slaves back to China. You come along with me— Mu-Piang show you where Dlagon hide!"

Without waiting for permission then, Mu-Piang heaved to his feet and beckoned with a thin long hand, whose nails were inches long, guarded by shields of jade and silver. Wentworth's eyes were half-closed. How long did he have now? Ten minutes, five perhaps. The pain in his breast was a tearing agony. The orchid was bursting its confines. His breath came in short, panting gasps. There wasn't enough air in the world to fill his lungs, but his brain... It was working at last!

Mu-Piang might indeed lead him to the Dragon, but it would be by devious paths, unless he determined to plunge the Spider into one of the myriad traps that studded these underground warrens. And there wasn't time... An idea was hammering at Wentworth's temples; something that had been there a long time and had struggled for lucid expression; an idea... Wentworth drove himself to his feet. He did not have the strength now to force his way to the Dragon, but there was another way.

He knew there was, if only it would come to the front of his brain. It had to do with those slaves of the Dragon....

Mu-Piang's figure was wavering before the Spider's eyes. He could see the carven, wrinkled face and it seemed to retreat, then to surge toward him in the half-darkness of the corridor. And then he saw the gun in Mu-Piang's hand! Wentworth's shot was not even ordered by his brain; it was not necessary, so long had the perfection of his gun-fire been consigned to the reflexes of his powerful body. But even as he fired, he felt a powerful blow that hurled him to the floor, felt the numbing fire of a wound through his side. But as he fell, he saw Mu-Piang's face shattered by his own lead; saw the Chinese sent looping backward by the impact.

A GREAT peacefulness seemed to settle over Wentworth, supine upon the earthen floor of the corridor. There was a moment of ease from the writhing, prodding pain in his breast. His brain... A hoarse cry pushed itself from Wentworth's throat! God, he should have seen it hours before, when he had stood bewildered over the bodies of the men the Dragon had promised to enslave—men from whose chests the red flower of the orchid had thrust, as even now, horribly, a living thing was working its way out through his own vitals.

If the Dragon planned to enslave those scientists, it could not be through death. Even the Dragon's great powers could not summon resurrection. But it would be an *apparent* resurrection. The orchid then, did not kill. It brought on a catalepsy from which the Dragon could revive his victims! It had to be that. God, it had to... *Nita!* Wentworth realized that he was already on his feet and stumbling back through Mu-Piang's shop, toward the street. Yes, it had to be that. This orchid in his breast would produce a death-like sleep from which he might be revived. *Might* be. It was for the Dragon to determine whether he should awaken or die!

Wentworth was in the street. His car... Somehow, he was at the wheel, hurling the machine through New York's traffic. Lights he ignored. Miraculously, his body seemed to gain strength from that wound in his side. It might be that it weakened the dreadful plant within him, slowed its action. It could slow his brain. In that swift moment, his thoughts were unbelievably clear. He could phone Kirkpatrick now and warn him of what threatened, that the ships of the harbor were to be seized. But if he did that, all those men who had fallen under the insidious blooming of the orchid would die! They must be first revived by the Dragon. Afterward Wentworth must free them!

For a moment, Wentworth was shaken by doubts. It was pure theory, his guess about the orchid. Suppose he should be wrong! Did he have the right to withhold his information from Kirkpatrick? No, damn it, he was right! He *had* to be! And he was right about another thing, too. The Dragon had threatened him personally with enslavement. The Dragon's men would come for him, too, and for Nita....

The pain was throbbing terribly through his body again. Coughing shook him so that he could scarcely see, but still he drove the car at top speed toward his home. That was where the Dragon would seek him, and he must not seek in vain! Fumblingly, Wentworth reached out for the stimulants without which he never traveled, since he could not tell when wounds might lay him low. He found the vial of powerful fluid, and yet he hesitated. Stimulants might only hurry the work of this thing within him. Once he had fallen into the trance of the orchid, stimulants might help....

His thoughts came fumblingly now, with the heaviness of stumbling, leaden feet. He gripped the stimulant in his hand and sped on and on. Sutton Place... What already? There were blue-coated police leaping out to stop him. Laughter pumped at Wentworth's lungs: laughter terribly broken by coughs. He whirled the car on two wheels into the dead-end street on which the protective walls of his fortified mansion fronted. There was a steel gate there which would open to precisely timed sonics.

Somehow, Wentworth dragged out a tiny silver whistle and piped its two notes into the shouting furor of the blockading, pursuing police. Timing... He could not even see his watch, but he had sounded the pipes so many times. He blew the signal and drove the car straight at the steel gates.

Miraculously, he found himself inside as the powerful mechanism of the gates, provided for just such an emergency, whipped the gates open. He heard the hollow clang as they slammed shut again. The police would not dare to breach those walls. They knew how well they were protected with electricity and hidden mines. At least, they would await word from Kirkpatrick and he knew that word would not be given. No, he was safe inside here—safe from the police, but not from the Dragon. Somehow, the Dragon had made an entrance and would come again. Wentworth hoped he would come. If not... If not, then this was the end of the Spider; the end of Nita, and perhaps of the people for whom he had fought so long and faithfully. But Wentworth's decision was made. He could not change it....

WENTWORTH STAGGERED into the small automatic elevator that would carry him up to the third floor where Nita lay, and darkness swam before his eyes. The vial was still clutched tightly in his hand—the vial of stimulant that he dared not take, while the orchid still burgeoned within him—that he would not be able to take after it had flowered. Why, the elevator had *stopped!* Wentworth saw that the door stood open before him. He staggered out, reeled along the corridor toward the drawing-room. Yes, Nita still was there—sweet Nita with that horrid bloom on her breast. It seemed a little wilted now. It seemed....

Wentworth was beside Nita once more, staring down at her, and strangely, at last, he was aware of the tears on his face—streaming down now, burning his cheeks, stinging his eyes. Strange that he could feel such little things amid the hell of pain that drew his muscles, that shook him with the awful ague of approaching death. Fumblingly, he uncorked the vial and held it to Nita's lips. He could not take it now; but there was a chance it might save Nita. Just a chance.... He thrust the vial between her parted lips and his hand fell limply back to his side. A gust of pain doubled him up so that he slid to his knees.

It was the end. Within moments, that flower would bloom on his chest as the Dragon had foretold; and Wentworth would plunge into the deathlike sleep. Sleep? But God, he could not be sure! Suppose he were wrong! Suppose the eagerness of the hopes which he held for Nita, of hearing her sweet laughter and the love-huskiness of her voice, had misled him! Suppose this were not catalepsy, but... but death itself!

Pain bowed Wentworth to the floor. His knees were drawn to his chest and the sweat of agony stood out on him, like great salty tears—as if all his body, all that he was, would weep for Nita, dead. If he were wrong... A groan of pure agony was wrung from Wentworth, an expression of pain that not all his physical suffering could force from his brave heart. *If he were wrong....*

Those pain-contorted limbs straightened incredibly. Like a dead man moving, Wentworth dragged himself across the floor. He knew suddenly that he was wrong; that there would be no resurrection. He must warn Kirkpatrick of the plans that the demon Dragon had laid. At least that much he could accomplish. He crawled across the room and reached for the phone with clawed hands. He spoke, shouted, pleaded into the telephone... and finally to his brain, that only his mighty will had kept alive, came the realization that... *that the wire was cut!*

Rage jerked him to his feet and for a long instant, Wentworth stood rigidly, his head thrown back, defiant even in this moment of ultimate doom. Then his clawed hands, pain-driven, lifted to his chest and ripped aside the cloth that seemed to strangle him. Straight and stiff as a tree he plunged to the floor and, from the scarred flesh of his chest, a tiny green shoot like the head of a vicious snake thrust its way to unfold slowly, in awful beauty, the Orchid of Blood....

CHAPTER 11
NIGHTMARE DOOM

T HE INTOLERABLE pain that had hurled Nita van Sloan to the couch seemed to have no end. If there was a period when blackness intervened she did not know it. Only finally, there seemed to be a rhythm of pain, a rapid rhythm that might almost be the beating of her heart; that *was* the beating of her heart. Each throb of it seemed to pulse fresh agony through her reluctant body. It eased finally, and she realized that she still was supine upon a softness that at first she mistook for the same couch.

She opened her eyes and saw a low ceiling and, across from her, a large round window beyond which she could see only a low, gray sky. It was some minutes before she understood that the round window was a porthole—that the movement of the room was actual and represented the rolling pitch of a ship at sea!

Nita closed her eyes again and tried to rationalize her situation, and dimly she perceived something of the thing that had happened. The pain, she thought, had been some drug which had overcome her and now, a prisoner, she was being borne to sea. That could only mean one thing—*the Dragon had her in his power!*

The actual phrasing of that thought hurled Nita from the bunk in which she lay. But her legs were pitifully weak. They gave under her and pitched her to the floor and for long moments, on hands and knees, she crouched there and gathered her strength.

Finally, by gripping the side of the bunk, she got to her feet and, bracing herself on the wall, moved toward the porthole through which now, she could see the gray and sullen sea.

Aft, she could make out another steamer and beyond that a third and a fourth in a long, staggered line across the heaving ocean. But there was no glimpse of land. Nita gripped her temples and tried to think. She couldn't know, that with drugged, subservient crews, these ships were bearing the slaves and stolen wealth of the Dragon to safety! She was conscious only of a dull pain that was like a weakness in her chest and there was a fogginess upon all her thoughts. But her strength was returning momentarily. Where was Dick, and what was the meaning of this strange abduction? For a minute, terror gnawed at her control. She wanted to fling herself against these confining walls; to do anything rather than stay here passively and wait for the horror that must lie ahead.

Nita turned her back on the porthole and, with fumbling steps, managed to make her way across the small cabin toward the door. She had no hope that she would find it unlocked, but it was madness not to make the attempt. As she had guessed, the knob resisted her strongest effort to turn it and the exertion left her weak and trembling. She stood rigidly, forcing herself to breathe slowly and deeply—resolutely closed her mind to horror. What she must do, obviously, was regain her strength as rapidly as possible.

She was ravenously hungry, but that must wait. Meantime, movement, not repose, was what she needed. She set herself to pacing the floor, back and forth, back and forth. Gradually, as she had hoped, the shakiness went out of her limbs and the tremor from her breast. It was when she was near the door that she heard the hissing laughter of the Dragon!

For an instant, she was frozen in terror, then she ran softly to the bunk and threw herself supine upon it. What lay ahead, she could only conjecture, painfully. But the more she knew before she was forced to face the Dragon, the better chance she would have of escape. Sardonic mirth twisted her lips, and what was close to a sob of despair swelled in her throat. Dear God, what hope….

It required an incredible exertion of will to master her emotion before the rasping of the lock told her that the Dragon was entering her cabin! She caught the faint sibilance of his walk and the sharp thud of a woman's heels, entering with him! "**SHE LIVES!**" cried the woman, and Nita recognized the voice as that of the one whom the Chinese had called the Blood Orchid! "She lives! I was given to understand that she would be allowed to die! Master, I who have served you faithfully—I who am your slave—cry for a boon! Give me this woman's life."

Nita heard the words without any emotion other than a rising hatred for this woman whom, always, she had seen amid scenes of horror. And she knew what motive actuated the woman now. She dreaded that the Dragon would become… interested… in Nita. Nita scarcely repressed a shudder of horror as she heard the sibilance of the Dragon's laughter.

"Fear not, my orchid," the Dragon replied harshly. "I want her only for utilitarian purposes. She will be helpful in subduing a stubborn slave. A very stubborn slave…" The voice was directly over Nita now and only the iron control that Wentworth had taught her through long hours of practice permitted her to maintain her posture of coma—to keep her breathing steady and her eyes naturally closed. But if he should touch her!

"I have here," came the woman's voice again, "a vial of the orchid blood. Let me administer it to her, so that you can question her about the plans that the Spider laid. We must talk for you. It will only take a moment…."

By the approaching nearness of the woman's voice, Nita knew that she was bending close over her, that the vial was nearing her lips… She heard a sudden gasp of pain, then the Dragon's voice.

"Would you kill her anyway, despite my orders, my Orchid?" it asked softly. "You know as well as I that the orchid blood administered too soon brings death! You are not very obedient, my deadly little flower. Be careful lest I find some other woman more suitable to my needs. Be careful, beautiful little one."

A low moan of pain came from the woman and Nita risked the slight opening of her eyes that would give her a glimpse through her lowered lashes at the tableau before her. The orchid woman had cringed to her knees beneath the grip of the Dragon's and the nail-guards that were like fantastically beautiful claws gouging into the soft flesh of her pale throat.

"Mercy, master!" the woman begged hoarsely, lifting her white stricken face. "Mercy, master! I did but seek to help thee! It was my zealousness…."

"Your jealousy!" prompted the Dragon gently.

The woman muffled a scream as the claws brought forth a

thread of blood from her flesh. "My jealousy!" she conceded brokenly. "Yes, lord! My jealousy! My love for thee!"

The Dragon claw lifted from her throat then, and the horrid, hissing laughter came again. "Remember, my little flower," he said, "that I have the means of extracting truth, and remember my orders. This woman is to live so that I may conquer this stubborn Spider...."

"Your drugs!" the woman pleaded, shrinking to her feet. "Your powerful will! Surely, these are enough to subdue any Westerner!"

"Enough," the Dragon acknowledged. "Yes, enough. But under my drugs and my will, he would not suffer. One who has deprived the so must suffer! Come!"

THE FOOTSTEPS of the two beat a slow retreat across the room and Nita, watching through her lashes, saw the Dragon turn at the door and stare back at her. Almost she could see the eyes that burned behind that awful skull face which hid his countenance, and what she saw was horrible. She knew now how the Dragon intended Wentworth to suffer! Horror convulsed Nita and, as the door closed, she flung once more from the bunk. She must escape, now....

Her eyes swung to the porthole. She could squeeze through that, but though she was an expert swimmer, she knew that she could not long survive in that sea. Better that... A thousand times better that than the fate that lay before her at the hands of this Chinese beast!

Swiftly, her breath coming drily in her throat, Nita wrenched at the screw that held the port-hole glass shut against the storm.

It was only when the glass had swung wide, when she was look-ing about for some object on which to climb that memory stopped her in her tracks. Memory of the Dragon's words... *"so that I may conquer this stubborn Spider..."* Suddenly, the meaning dawned upon her. He did not speak of capturing the Spider, but of subduing him. In heaven's name, Dick also was a prisoner on this hell ship!

It was in this same moment that she saw the stealthy turning of the doorknob, and her eyes flew about the narrow confines of her cabin. No weapon here; nothing with which to defend herself. She did not even question whose hand might be turning that knob. She knew. There would be no need for the Dragon to come thus furtively.

No, the orchid woman had returned to murder her! That was the only possible solution!

Nita forced herself to calmness. Ordinarily, she would dread battle with no woman alive. One of the things that Wentworth had taught her of necessity, when she had determined to join her fate with his, was the art of self-defense. Everything that Wentworth could teach her, she knew. But she was weakened by whatever drug had been pumped into her veins....

With a tiger-like leap, Nita seized the blanket from her bunk and crossed to the wall beside the door. It was opening now, with a slow caution that bespoke the terror of the woman who thus defied the Dragon!

The woman slipped into the room, her eyes concentrated on the door while she eased it shut. The instant it closed, Nita sprang like a panther upon her back, whipping the blanket tightly over her head, binding her arms to her sides with all her wiry strength. But if she had thought to overwhelm the woman in that first instant, Nita had underestimated the Orchid. As suddenly as she attacked, the Orchid was equally quick. She dropped to her knees, and Nita barely avoided being thrown heavily by the drag on her arms. She jerked up her knee and jarred the Orchid's head forward, but she missed the exact nerve center for which she aimed—or else the blanket muffled the blow.

The Orchid rolled away, whipped the blanket from her head and faced Nita across the width of the narrow cabin, a slim needle of a dagger in her right hand.

The Orchid woman's mouth twisted in a thin smile, "You shall sleep again, white fool!" she whispered. "And this time, forever! With you gone, the Dragon can turn to no one but me. Do you understand that? Do you...."

As she spoke, she was creeping forward as a cat creeps, the knife powerfully poised. Nita feigned fear and cringed against the wall. With the blanket gone, she had no weapon at all except her wits. Her greatest hope now was to make the Chinese think that she would have an easy victory.

"Please!" she whispered. "Please, I do not want to die! I only thought it was the Dragon whom I hate. Just let me get away! Take me to the man I love, the Spider, and let us get away now together!"

In the woman's total lack of surprise, Nita recognized that her guess was all too true. Dick was a prisoner here aboard this boat, probably wrapped in the same drugged slumber that had held her.

"Fool!" said the Orchid. "How could you escape? You are far out to sea, you and all the other slaves that the Master carries back to the East to serve him; to help him conquer the West…" Nita knew that she was talking more to distract her from the threat of that knife which was being slowly drawn back for a throw; and the words came with such a shock that the purpose almost succeeded.

Nita realized in the woman's brief phrases that these ships racing across the gray seas were carrying with them the human beings whom the Dragon had said he intended to seize; the scientists of Albany and Pittsboro… And Dick was helpless!

Her startled eyes saw the woman's knife wrist whip forward in a throw that it seemed impossible to avoid. Nita did not attempt to move her body aside, but staked all her hopes, her very life, on a swift parry that Dick had taught her. Her quick left hand swept through the air and the swift-moving palm struck the dagger, hurled it aside just in time. It struck the wall with a flat, vicious thud.

Instantly, the Chinese woman was lunging toward her to seize the blade, stooping. Nita did not try to grab it, but, as the woman came toward her, she leaped forward and struck.

An out-thrust foot caught the Orchid's ankle and the stiffened edge of Nita's right hand cut down across the back of the woman's neck. There was a muffled cry, and the Orchid pitched forward. Her limbs jerked convulsively, the toes of her spike-heeled shoes drumming the floor. Nita stared down at her incredulously. Through too cruel experience, she knew what those tremors portended. But it was impossible that she had killed the Orchid woman with that blow, shrewd as it had been!

Frantically, Nita flung down on her knees beside the woman, spun her over on her back. With a choked cry of horror then, Nita sprang to her feet, her knuckles pressed against her teeth. With lithe quickness, the Orchid Woman had succeeded in reaching the dagger with her hand, just as Nita's blow fell. Her whole weight had driven her body down upon the needle point of that blade. It was buried to the hilt in her breast!

FOR A long, horror-shocked moment, Nita stood rigid, staring down at the dead body of the lovely woman. Then she knotted her fists at her side and forced herself to calm. She had not deliberately slain the woman, though her own life had been at stake. She could not let shock overwhelm her. Nita's cheeks were stiff with the effort it cost, but she bent over the Orchid Woman and laboriously dragged her to the bunk, flung her upon it.

She forced herself then to search the woman's body, to find the vial of orchid blood, which, if given at the right time, could revive a victim from the coma of the drug that had been administered, which could revive Dick....

Nita carefully covered the Orchid Woman's body with the blanket and crept toward the door. The knob turned easily in her hand and she peered out into a corridor that was wholly deserted. Her heart was beating violently high in her throat. She knew that not only her own life was at stake, but that of the man to whom she gave her love—and of all those whom the Dragon had enslaved. With that knowledge, she fought against her fears and crept out into the corridor....

She had gone no more than twenty feet when the sound of men's voices came to her ears and she darted down a short cross-corridor, crouched there motionless while she waited. Her straining ears caught the word "prisoners" and then the footsteps faded forward along the passageway she had been following. For other long seconds, Nita hid herself before she dared to approach the hall from which she had fled. She began to slip forward then in the direction the men had taken. It was her guess that they were on their way to the prisoners.

Hours seemed to drag past while she made her swift and silent way along the corridor and, at long last, she caught the sound of voices again and recognized that it came from the cabins at her right. And the voices were suddenly louder. Even as Nita identified the direction from which they came, she saw a doorknob begin to turn! There was no time for thought, scarcely time to act. Nita thrust at the door beside her, and it yielded, let her into a half-dark cabin. She heard a man's angry, disturbed voice, then an oath of surprise.

Nita wheeled to see a seaman rearing up from the bunk, saw his eyes brighten with surprise, and delight. Nita's teeth clenched together. For a few moments, she must keep him silent.

"You must be quiet," she whispered, "or I'll have to go!"

The man's grin broadened. He heaved himself from the bunk and, in that instant, Nita saw her chance. She leaped forward and, with all her weight behind the blow, drove the bent knuckles of her right hand against his larynx! With a choked gasp, he flopped back on the bunk. His hands clasped his throat. Nita struck again, this time on nerve centers below the ear, as Wentworth had taught her. The seaman shivered and straightened out, unconscious.

Now Nita was back at the door, listening. No sound came to her ears and, moments later, she opened the door a crack to peer into the corridor. Silence there—emptiness. Quickly then, she crossed the hallway and tried the opposite door—the one through which the men had come. It yielded under her hand and she darted inside. Long rows of bunks met her eyes and, on each one, a man lay motionless!

Nita pressed her shoulders against the door, waited; but no one moved. Her quick eyes darted over the line of recumbent men and a reassuring sight caught her gaze. To each bunk was affixed a board with a clip which held a sheet of paper in place. No need to wonder what they were; hospital charts! She remembered what the Dragon had said then about too quick administration of the drug she carried in her hand. She ran to the nearest bunk and consulted the chart, saw the indications of past treatments, the orders for future medicines. Nita drew in a long sigh of relief.

The last obstacle was removed then, her lack of knowledge of the drug. If only she could find Dick….

A trembling seized Nita. She could not tell how much time she had. At any moment, the Dragon might start a search for the Orchid Woman or invade Nita's own room for her! If they came too soon….

"Dick!" Nita muffled her cry. "Oh, *Dick!*"

She flung herself down on her knees and clasped his still face between her hands. He lay as cold, as motionless as death itself. With eager eyes, she scanned the chart attached to the side of his bunk, then her eyes leaped to the great clock at the end of the room. In twenty minutes, Wentworth was due to receive the orchid blood treatment. In twenty minutes! But in that time, it might be too late! She might be found, or the Dragon's men might make Wentworth a prisoner before then! Yet, the Dragon had said that to administer the orchid blood too soon meant certain death!

Nita gripped the vial in her hand and her eyes fixed with a tearful intensity on Dick's face. Their one chance… yet it might bring only death! Far off, Nita heard a hoarse shout, and then the tramping of many feet! It could mean only one thing. Her escape was discovered!

"God," she whispered. "God give me the strength to choose right!"

CHAPTER 12
END OF AN EMPIRE!

ALMOST IMMEDIATELY, it seemed to Nita, they found her huddled there beside Wentworth's bunk and yanked her to her feet. Without ceremony, she was thrust across the room. She managed to check herself at the door, get a last look back at Dick's white, still face. For all she knew, it might be the last time she would ever gaze on that face she loved so well.

Her Chinese captors brooked no delay. They thrust her violently out into the corridor and harried her along to the main cabin.

For an instant, Nita had the crazy illusion that once more she was back in the underground throne room where first she had seen the Dragon. She was bent viciously to the floor, her head rapped in a thrice-repeated kowtow. Then, as on that other occasion, the coolies drew back and left her, face to face, with the skull-faced figure upon its scarlet-petaled Buddha throne.

And the Dragon laughed softly, "You are a fit mate for the Emperor of the World," the hissing syllables beat slow time against Nita's brain. "Proud, loyal to the last. And not afraid to kill when there is need for it!"

"The woman deserved killing," she replied, and made her voice cold. "She came to poison me."

The Dragon chuckled in approbation. "I only quarrel with your methods, my dear, but perhaps you will learn. Our enemies should die, certainly, but they should die *slowly*. They should afford us the maximum of pleasure before they die. I shall show you how my enemies die, Nita, my dear, so that you may be worthy of me."

The Dragon lifted his hands.

"Revive the prisoner, Wentworth," he ordered. "And send me my executioners! Then let Wentworth be brought!"

Nita closed her eyes slowly, her face white as death itself. Her lips moved, but it was in prayer. She heard the hissing mockery of the Dragon's laughter, and the rustling of the silken curtains as the coolies moved to carry out his orders. She forced her eyes open, forced herself to gaze upon the beast upon the orchid throne. If she could only manage to kill him....

The Dragon struck his palms together again and his voice hissed softly, terribly across the room. "You keep me waiting, I believe!" he hissed. "You keep the Dragon waiting...."

"Master!" the coolie screeched. "Master, the one who is called the Spider, has risen from the dead! He is gone! Disappeared!"

Nita threw back her head and laughter poured from her throat, gay, exultant laughter. "Thank you, God!" she cried softly. "Thank you for helping me to choose right!"

The Dragon's skull face was turned toward her and she could feel the stab of those awful eyes.

"Send me my executioners," he said softly.

THE COOLIE sprang to his feet and backed from the room, the thud of his fugitive feet beating their retreat along the deck. But Nita knew that there were others, many others, behind the curtains.

The smile lingered on her lips. Nothing mattered now. Dick was free. It did not matter that the boat was alive with hostile men, nor that he was unarmed. Dick's quick mind would find a way. She knew that he would. Her smile tautened a little on her lips.

"I understand now," the Dragon whispered. "The vial of orchid blood that my Orchid carried. You stole it and risked giving it to your lover before the time was ripe. It may interest you to know, woman, that the effect of too early potion is this—the victim recovers consciousness and, within the course of fifteen minutes afterward, *dies!*"

"Four minutes have passed—are you ready, executioner?"

Nita smothered the scream that surged to her lips, her eyes staring horrified at the Dragon. Was he lying? Was he saying this to rob her of hope?

"So your lover's escape will mean nothing," the Dragon went on calmly. "Nothing at all. But I permit no trickery of myself. You understand that? You tricked me, and for that there is a penalty..." Once more gray light struck across the room, cold, cold. "Ah, here are my executioners."

Nita felt her muscles loosen, her mouth go dry with apprehension. Hands seized her roughly, bowed her to her knees and ripped her dress from her shoulders. Beside her head, she saw the point of a headsman's great sword.

"Announce over the emergency loud-speaker system," said the Dragon gently, "that I shall wait five minutes for the Spider to surrender himself. If he has not appeared here at the end of that time, the headsman shall strike off his woman's head!"

Nita closed her eyes with a small prayer that Dick would not hear, but the loud squawking of the loudspeakers killed that hope. Then she prayed that he would not come....

"Two minutes have passed," the Dragon announced, his voice purring, soft.

Nita opened her eyes and lifted her head slowly. She could see the red sash of the headsman and, strangely, hidden behind it was an automatic pistol. Hope gasped dizzily into her heart. If she could get that gun... but her hands had been bound tightly behind her. She turned her head a fraction of an inch. On each side of her were the bare, braced feet of the executioners. When the moment came, they would step away from her, the great sword would flash upward....

"Three minutes have passed," purred the Dragon.

Nita strained against the cords that bit into her wrists and they only tore more deeply into her flesh. She persisted, working on them desperately, but they would not yield. Something very like a sob strained at Nita's throat. In God's name, where was Dick? No, no, she did not want him to come. It would only mean his death. Surely, the entrances of this room were lined with men waiting for him to enter so that they could set upon and slay him.

"Four minutes have passed! Are you ready, executioner?"

The man with the heavy sword grunted unintelligibly and the sword lifted past Nita's head. No longer could she see that ominous, razor-keen blade. She felt a wet tracery across the back of her neck and an uncontrollable shudder passed over her. It was thus the executioners of China marked the spot where the blade should shear. Tears squeezed out of Nita's eyes, but she did not lift her head, did not plead for mercy. She asked only that Dick would not come. Let him, at least, be saved. God grant that the Dragon had lied about the poison qualities of the orchid blood....

"Five minutes! Spider, come forth!"

There was no answer and Nita closed her eyes. Her teeth were set on her lower lip. Oh, give her courage now; courage for just a few seconds more. It would not be long....

"Executioner!"

Nita felt the cold touch of steel upon the back of her neck as

165

the swordsman took his gauge of the stroke. Then unaccountably, the steel brushed down her back and she felt its cold kiss upon her wrists, between them, felt her bonds part. She went rigid with bewilderment.

"Spider, come forth!" the Dragon trumpeted. *"One second more. Executioner... ready. Spider, come forth!"*

The voice that answered came, incredibly, from just over Nita's head. "Were you calling for me, Dragon?" The voice was cool, arrogant, sure, and a moment later, a tiny whisper dropped to Nita's waiting ear, a whisper in the voice she knew and loved. *Dick!*

"An automatic behind my sash, Nita," he whispered. "When I give the word, shoot. Empty the clip into the Dragon!"

THE SWORD swished through the air. Nita heard its high, lethal whine and the brief startled shout of the Chinese who stood on the other side of her. But it got no farther than that. A body thudded to the rug. Nita's hands were free of the cords that had bound them and she lifted one, furtively, toward the automatic on Wentworth's thigh. She touched it, but her hands could not close on the butt—her hand was numb!

A frantic cry welled in Nita's throat. She tried to force movement, action, feeling into that hand by her will, and she could not! Agonizedly, she whispered to Dick....

The Dragon was laughing, "A nice tableau, Spider," he rasped, "and nicely timed. I suppose you killed my idiot headsman? Yes, I thought so, and your disguise is clever. *No, don't move, Wentworth—or you die!"* Nita's frightened eyes saw a revolver in the

Dragon's hand now, its muzzle held unwaveringly upon Wentworth's heart! Her hand wouldn't come to life—*it wouldn't!*

Wentworth rested the point of the sword on the floor and leaned both forearms on its hilt. The blade made a wide shield for his thigh, behind which Nita might reach the automatic, if her fingers would only work again. Some little life was returning to them, but it wasn't enough. When she pulled that trigger, she had to be very, very sure... or the Dragon would live to kill Dick!

"It seems," Wentworth said quietly, "that I considerably reduced your force of men in the battle for the government's gold, Dragon. You've got them watching the deck and the corridors for my return, haven't you, Dragon? You never dreamed I was right in the room with you. Just, Dragon, as you do not dream that you are doomed, even as you sit on that fool throne!"

He continued. "No, it doesn't matter in the least if you kill me. You see, I figured out long ago who you were, and I imparted that bit of information to Kirkpatrick before I left!"

The Dragon's breath made a hissing sound in the barren jaws of the skull face, "You lie!" he said thickly. "You lie! Kirkpatrick is mad, by this time. I have robbed him of reason!"

Wentworth laughed aloud. Nita saw that he swayed his thigh slightly so that the automatic swung a little toward her. She bit her lips, wrung her hand in an effort to restore circulation and feeling. Plainly, Dick was playing for time—time for her to act. And she could not!

"That was what you thought, Dragon," he said calmly. "What happened is this. I shocked Kirkpatrick out of your control. A psychic shock, Dragon, the only thing that could work. I told everything before I left. At this moment, the navy is scouring the seas for you. Planes will put out as soon as the heavens clear a little. And they will know whom they want. No disguise will hide you now."

"Enough of this talking," said the Dragon harshly. He lifted his voice, started to call his men.

"Don't!" Wentworth said softly. "Don't if you want to live to see your men enter this room! Don't call your coolies, *Fu-Chang!*"

An inarticulate snarl jerked at the body on the throne chair. The gun reached out....

"Aren't you curious," Wentworth asked calmly, "how I happened to penetrate your identity? But it was very simple, really, Fu-Chang! You knew when you hit upon this scheme for world domination that you would have to eliminate the Spider, so you prepared to do that at the very first. I was almost taken in by the disaster that overtook your daughter, Hwang-yo. But you had only planned for the orchid to flower in her breast—a thing you could easily counter-act. It was no part of your plans that I should carry her into the acid chamber!"

He went on. "But for the fact that I did not know for so long the truth about the Blood Orchid—that it did not actually kill—I should have guessed long ago. It always puzzled me, Fu-Chang, that any enemy could invade your myriad passage-ways without being overpowered. Your traps were too terrible, too effective to permit that! Yet enemies had broken in—and set up other traps in their turn! Traps that would have taken hours to prepare! Really, quite simple, Fu-Chang. Not court evidence, but enough to send Kirkpatrick on your trail. He will see to it that there is no need of a court trial, Fu-Chang!"

The Dragon seemed calmer now. With a quick hand, he stripped off the skull mask and his twisted, bitterly hostile face showed.

"You are lying, of course, Wentworth," Fu-Chang said quietly. "I know of your visit to Kirkpatrick, but his activities afterward showed no sign that he knew my identity. It was thirty-six hours later before we put out to sea and reduced sailors and passengers to the slavery of my drugs. No, Wentworth, I have only to kill you and it will be victory! Victory for me and for my race when we return."

The gun reached out and, in purely Western and scientific way, Fu-Chang, the Dragon, sighted the revolver at Wentworth's heart. "It is not the way I would choose," he said quietly, "but necessity, not I, dictates the way!"

Wentworth was rigidly braced. "Now, Nita!" he whispered. *"Now!"*

Nita's still half-numbed hand ripped the automatic from its holster and in the same instant she fired. A sob of despair gasped from her, for, even as she pulled the trigger, she knew that she had missed! Fu-Chang gave a start and his own bullet went wild, too. He had time for no second shot. The great headsman's sword leaped and swung, sailed through the air in a whistling, deadly spiral. Fu-Chang screamed once... and then the sword's blade slashed home. And the throne of the Blood Orchid now was empty! Fu-Chang was dead....

IN A swoop, Wentworth had the automatic in Nita's hand and

was bounding toward the doors, but with the loss of their leader, the Chinese were completely cowed. Obediently, they allowed themselves to be herded into locked cabins—and, afterward, Wentworth set about reviving the scientist slaves who still lay in the coma of the Blood Orchid in the bunks below; summoned the drugged and will-less crew and issued orders to put back to New York harbor. The other steamers obediently executed turns and followed in the wake of the ship the Spider had recaptured.

And as the boat picked up speed on the homeward course, the gray skies broke in the west, let through a last slanting red ray of sunset. Wentworth paused for a moment in his work over the captive scientists to stare into that promising ray of light. Nita's hand came gently to his arm and he turned to smile into her upturned face.

"It's over, dear," he said softly. "Tomorrow night, we'll be back home again. We can even drop in on a show on Broadway...."

Nita tried to smile, but her lips remained a little drawn, after so much horror. Her answer was desperately gay.

"And you can send me flowers...."

Her voice choked and her eyes widened a little at a thought that would haunt her to her death. "Flowers, Dick, but no... no orchids."